CHI'S

Advance Praise

"Chi the Antelope King's Epic Journey Home *is a stirring and delightful story that captures the imagination, even as it opens our eyes to important truths about human behavior. Brilliantly written and beautifully illustrated, this book will appeal to everyone, young and old."*— **Neal D. Barnard, MD, FACC, President, Physicians Committee for Responsible Medicine**

"Truth and justice are written in such a beautiful way that when you read this work of art you will be forever changed. To rid the world of power and greed is possible if we all embrace the powerful message from Chi, the young king of the roan antelope population. Alex's message is clear; one peaceful world for all, human and nonhuman alike. With stunning illustrations and wonderful words of wisdom on every page, this book is a must for everyone." —**Marlene Watson-Tara, teacher, author, and co-founder of Human Ecology Project and MACROVegan**

"Chi's Journey is a wonderful, adventurous book and reads like a powerful dream. Like Odysseus' travels in the Odyssey after ransacking Troy, we are guided to follow the journey of Chi and his animal friends through the historical Five Peaceful Civilizations as well as the reality of the present world, where animals are 'simply cogs in the food chain or factory farm assembly lines.' In this powerful dream, the reader can enjoy Jack's poetic

language and see the strength of the animals working together as a team, remaining free and in harmony with their environment. The story demonstrates the generosity of animals in forgiving the injustices inflicted on them by us humans."—**Abraham Oort, former Climate Scientist at Princeton University and author of** *Living on Earth*

"*A global fable, Chi is a masterpiece in art and words. We follow this 'hero's journey' around the world with a small group of majestic animals. We discover important spiritual truths along the way revealed with the help of gods and spirits. Support is provided by animal and human friends when a most surprising transformation offers hope to all.*"—**Cynthia Vann, author** *Humanity at a Wireless Crossroads*

"*Alex Jack does it again, this time in a mythical epic about a world that could one day be. Both young and mature audiences can enjoy this contemporary account of character strength, mutual support, and the image of* shalom—*wholeness and completeness, understood simply as peace.*"—**Ginat Rice, co-founder and director,** *The Rice House, Israel*

"*Thirty years ago, Simba, a young lion prince, conveyed invaluable lessons about the human heart; ten years later, Nemo, an astute clownfish came to life for millions but neither the lion nor the fish addressed issues that now threaten life on earth as we know it. Algorithms fuel pervasive mechanistic intelligence that overwhelms everyday life, ultimately posing the existential question of survival. If words alone, citizen action, and conceptual thinking could have solved our problems, we would have reversed this trend a decade ago.*

"*In this remarkable tale for the ages, ancient voices worth listening to arrive in all shapes and sizes through the imagination, carrying the unspoken wisdom of sentient beings. We meet Chi, an antelope with timeless grace and powerful purpose walking the African savannah, a crane named Dao, and a bestie baboon called Thoth. With a condor, bat, butterfly, and rattlesnake among many others, these beautifully illustrated characters remind the reader of the challenges we all face.*

"*As we strive to honor nature rather than conquer it, this scholarly saga, written with heartfelt compassion and remarkable insight, allows readers of all ages to step away from an anthropocentric mindset just long enough to realize the beauty of the natural world and the magnificent interconnected-ness of all life forms. 'We must find a way to live together peacefully,' the antelope urges, and this poignant story is a potent reminder of that fundamental fact. Please enjoy!"*—**William Spear, Fortunate Blessings Foundation**

"In difficult times we all need fables. Giving voice to the spirit of animals reminds us of our kinship and place in nature. Alex Jack has given us a fable for these times, a reflection on how humankind has strayed off the course of harmony and how animals may again become the teachers. His band of animal heroes face human-made dangers with wisdom and a fresh perspective on both the past and the present. A lovely story with great illustrations and a message of love and unity. Give it a read, you will not regret it."—**Bill Tara, Co-Founder, Human Ecology Project, author, and teacher**

"Chi the Antelope King's Epic Journey Home takes us on a wild ride around the globe with a band of intrepid animals trying to make their way back from captivity to the wilderness. We follow them on their journey as they discover the depredation humanity has worked on the environment in the name of progress and learn what we need to do to heal our suffering planet. Alex Jack gives us a heart-rending but ultimately hopeful tale. Filled with myth and magic, it's a book to read with your children, and to set us all on a healthier, kinder path forward."—**Sachi Kato, mother, macrobiotic cooking teacher, and co-author of** *The One Peaceful World Cookbook*

"Imagine the entire sacred web of Life could speak! Imagine People had 'ears to hear and eyes to see all the pain and suffering' felt everywhere outside our efficiently built cities. Would we be praised as God's wise children, the compassionate and caring-for-all stewards of the Earth?! Or would we hear a loud and clear lament for our carelessness and complete disregard for the million-year-old, sacred connections and friendships? Then, imagine you could hear and see this all. How would you spend your days left on this beautiful Earth?! Well, read this book, it will make you think over! . . . but most of all, do what you can to make a difference!"—**Karel & Jarka Becvar-Adamcova, Macrobiotic teachers and founders of TampopoFoods.com and ReConnect2Earth**

Chi the Antelope King's Epic Journey Home

Alex Jack

Chi the Antelope King's Epic Journey Home

© 2024 text and illustrations designed by Alex Jack

All rights reserved. Printed in the United States of America. First Edition.

For further information on special sales, mail-order sales, wholesale distribution, translations, foreign rights, contact the publisher: Planetary Health/Amberwaves Press, PO Box 487, Becket MA 01223 • (413) 623-0012 • shenwa26@yahoo.com

ISBN 9798879957709

10 9 8 7 6 5 4 3 2

Frontispiece: Maat, the ancient Egyptian goddess of truth and justice

Illustration on p. 8 facing Contents: Chiwara, the West African culture-bearer and father of agriculture

"One touch of nature makes the whole world kin."
— Troilus and Cressida

In memory of my mother Esther, who enthralled me in childhood with the Doctor Doolittle books; of my father Homer who visited Dr. Albert Schweitzer in Africa and instilled within me the doctrine of Reverence for Life; of Michio and Aveline Kushi, my mentors; to my wife Danka, daughter Mariya, sister Lucy, and former wife Gale who helped me develop a deeper appreciation of nature; and in gratitude for all my animal companions

Contents

Foreword   11

1. The Abduction   13
2. The Escape   18
3. The Trek to the Desert Southwest   25
4. The Flight of the Monarchs   30
5. The Whispering Stones   34
6. Echoes of the Past   39
7. Songs of Freedom   43
8. Voices of the Ocean   47
9. Fire Dance Down Under   50
10. The Panda's Domain   53
11. The Dragon's Song   57
12. The Roof of the World   61
13. Echoes of an Ancient River   65
14. Blowing in the Wind   67
15. Whispers of Santorini   71
16. A Trial of Hearts   75
17. The Song of Homecoming   79

Afterword   82
About the Author   87

Cast of Characters

Gods and Spirits
Chiwara, West African semi-antelope culture-bearer who introduced farming
Maat, Egyptian goddess of truth and justice
Thunder, celestial buffalo
Quetzacoatl, feathered serpent
Celestial emu of Australia
Longwei, Chinese dragon
Naga, Himalayan guardian
Anubis, Egyptian guide to the Underworld

The Band of Animal Refugees
Chi, West African antelope king
Thoth, Egyptian hamadryas baboon
Dao, Chinese red-crowned crane
Blossom, Monarch butterfly
Lithe, Bolivian jaguar
Nunkeri, Australian kangaroo
Zhi, Yunnan horseshoe bat
Rumi, Abyssinian cat from Istanbul
Zeus, Cretan bull from Santorini

Human Allies
Sophia Wood, elder hippie
Hopi villagers
Carlos, a Mexican campesino
Honeycomb, Amazonian guide
Casarabe elder and tribe
Ecuadoran captain of the *Midnight Mariner*
Jomo Moussa, Kenyan eco captain of *The Eyewitness*
Australian Aboriginals
Mei, wise Sichuan elder
Mei Ling, Chinese activist
Claire Ireland, captain of *Light as a Feather* and its "illegal" migrants
And The Inferno, rock band

Helena Mireau, conservationist
Bambara dancers of Mali

Helpful Animal Friends
Amma, Chi's mother
Jasper, California coyote
Silver, Chinook salmon
Crown, desert bald eagle
Drizzle, black bear
Howl, grey wolf
Slither, rattlesnake
Great Horn, pronghorn
Dolly, llama in the Andes
Profunda, Mexican condor
Squeeze, giant anaconda
Streak, black spider monkey
Gargantua, Galapagos tortoise
Beak, elder finch
Stunning, gigantic manta ray
Magenta, scarlet flycatcher
Clutch, giant Pacific octopus
Li Wei, Chinese red panda
Kailas, Himalayan tiger
Namgyal, Tibetan snow leopard
Placid, Giza camel

Villains
Robert Ott, scientific researcher and animal abductor
Netjer Djew, monster covered with sterile seeds in the Underworld

Foreword

In my series of books *Spiral of History: The Arc That Bends Toward Justice, Peace & Love*, I call the great harmonious eras in the past the Five Peaceful Civilizations. My wife Danka and I visited the site of one of them, Santorini, several years ago. The Aegean Island was a main hub of the Minoans, and we marveled at the peaceful, artistic nature of their society. The other four peaceful civilizations are the Indus Sarasvati Valley in present-day Pakistan, the Niger River Valley in Mali, Norte Chico in Peru, and Ancestral Aboriginal in Australia. (The artwork on the right depicts a stylized mother antelope and child from West Africa that commemorates Chiwara, the antelope-headed deity, who introduced farming and culture to humankind.)

On that trip, we also visited Göbekli Tepe, Çatalhöyük, and Boncuklu Höyük in Anatolia, which deepened our awareness of the paleolithic and neolithic past. In these epochs, humans lived harmoniously with the natural world, reverenced animals and plants, and fashioned their societies to mirror the rhythms of the earth and sky. In each case, people observed a plant-based diet, cultivated music and the arts, and developed prosperous trade networks. All five great domains flourished for millennia without organized violence or war.

Each of these five civilizations ultimately succumbed to great earth changes (as in the volcano and tsunamis that destroyed the Minoans and the prolonged drought that marked the end of the Indus Sarasvati Valley and Norte Chico cultures) or genocide (as in Australia). They were succeeded by what I call the Eight Wrathful Civilizations: Sumerian, Egyptian, Israelite, Vedic India, Chinese, Greek and Roman, the Mexica (Aztec and Maya), and Inca. Along with magnificent art and wondrous technologies, their legacy includes monarchy, patriarchy, slavery, and war.

With the notable exception of short-lived Golden Ages presided over by Ashoka and Harsha in India, an animal-based agriculture and diet governed these eight great civilizations. Alas, their heirs in the form of the modern cattle culture, dairy lobby, and multinational sugar and beverage industries still shape and influence the world today. This unhealthy ultra-processed fare and way of life has given rise to surveillance capitalism, surveillance communism, and other forms of authoritarianism that sacrifice the diversity of the planet to ideology, prejudice and discrimination, and growing inequality.

In *Chi, the Antelope King's Epic Journey Home*, the animals visit the sites of the Five Peaceful Civilizations (as well as the Anatolian locales and smaller peaceful cultural oases in the Amazon, China, and Tibet) and experience echoes of their artistry, resourcefulness, and wisdom. They also visit contemporary sites where scientific and medical arrogance, genetic biopiracy, and corporate greed govern and impede them on their quest.

I hope readers of all ages will enjoy this present-day tale of animal resilience, interspecies cooperation, and a vision of enduring planetary health and peace.

Alex Jack
Prague
June 10, 2024

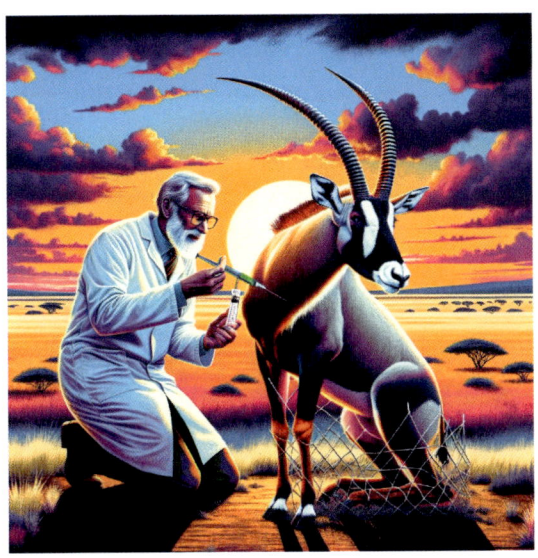

1. The Abduction

In the moonlit embrace of the West African savannah, Chi, the young king of the roan antelope population, stood proudly. His sleek, golden-brown fur shimmered under the moon's caress, and his regal horns, a testament to his lineage, gleamed. Chi's gaze swept over his domain, a kingdom of endless grasslands where life thrummed with an ancient rhythm.

As the herd grazed peacefully, Chi moved with a graceful confidence, his keen eyes surveying the vast expanse of the savannah. He carried the weight of responsibility upon his broad shoulders, for as king, it was his duty to ensure the safety and well-being of his subjects.

Little did Chi, the young monarch of his herd, know that the tranquility of this moonlit night would be shattered, setting into motion an odyssey that would transcend continents and challenge the very essence of his existence.

As the herd grazed peacefully under the starlit sky, a faint tremor, unnatural and foreboding, shattered the serenity. Chi's long tasseled ears twitched, and his muscles tensed. The sounds of the night, once familiar and comforting, were now drowned out by the clamor of engines and harsh human voices.

"Stay close," Chi murmured to Amma, his mother, whose wise eyes reflected the moonlight. The herd, sensing the unease of their king, gathered around him.

Suddenly, the tranquility was shattered by the rumble of approaching danger. Chi's senses tingled with instinctive warning, and he raised his head, ears perked in alertness. In the blink of an eye, the abductors struck, their nets casting a dark shadow over the moonlit landscape.

Unbeknownst to Chi, a group of scientific researchers led by Robert Ott, the steely King of the Field Zoologists, had descended upon the savannah, his eyes gleaming with pride in furthering medical research and free enterprise. His soul had been tarnished by greed, and he anticipated the bonus he would receive for this challenging assignment. Over the years, Ott had made the transition from a big-game hunter of exotic and endangered species for wealthy patrons to a master trafficker of rare birds, mammals, and marine life for zoos, science labs, and sanctuaries. Armed with digital technology that surpassed the wildest dreams of Chi or his ancestors, they operated with a cold precision that betrayed the ruthless efficiency of their trade.

In the blink of a digital eye, the kidnappers struck when their electronic sensors detected Chi's arrival at the riverbank. Surveillance satellites had profiled him as the strongest and swiftest of his kind and alerted his abductors who lay in wait. Nets soared through the air, expertly cast to entangle the unsuspecting antelope.

The moon bore witness to the tragedy unfolding beneath its silver gaze. Chi's eyes, wide with terror, locked onto those of his herd who managed to flee. His mother Amma, the matriarch of the herd, a wise and weathered doe, bleated in desperation as the poachers closed in, indifferent to the suffering they wrought upon her son.

Amidst the chaos of the ambush, Chi's instinct to protect his herd kicked into overdrive. He sprang into action, rallying his family to flee, his powerful hooves pounding against the earth in a desperate bid for escape. "To the river!" he commanded, his distinctive whistle carrying over the din. The herd surged forward, but Chi found himself ensnared, his struggle futile against the relentless grip of captivity.

In the chaos, Chi's world plunged into darkness. As Ott's white lab frocked figure approached, the glint of a tranquilizer dart held in gloved hands. As the substance coursed through Chi's veins, his vision blurred, and the once vibrant savannah faded into an inky void.

"We got him," Ott declared to his team in triumph, his eyes glinting with the prospect of wealth and professional recognition. Beside him, a new figure, Dr. Helena Mireau, a wildlife conservationist unwittingly entangled in Ott's schemes, watched with a mix of horror and fascination.

"Is this the only way?" Helena whispered, her voice barely audible over the sound of the struggling antelope.

Ott didn't answer, his attention fixed on Chi. The young monarch, even in defeat, held his head high, his eyes burning with an unquenchable fire of freedom.

As Chi was loaded into a container, the savannah seemed to hold its breath. Amma, her form receding into the night, let out a sorrowful cry that echoed the loss of the wild.

When consciousness returned, Chi found himself in a place unlike any he had ever known. The scent of unfamiliar foliage hung heavy in the air, and the ground beneath his hooves felt unnaturally solid. The plane flight in a cage across the Atlantic was a blur of darkness and despair for Chi. He awoke in a place where the sun was too bright, and the air carried the scent of confinement. Confusion gripped him as he surveyed his surroundings. This was no African savannah with its boundless freedom; it was a California safari park, a realm of illusionary freedom.

Slowly, it dawned on Chi that he was confined in a realm where the wild was tamed and put on display for the entertainment of humans. The sounds of laughter and chatter replaced the haunting calls of the African night, and Chi's heart sank as he realized the enormity of his captivity.

Amid this alien landscape, Chi found himself surrounded by other captives—creatures from distant corners of the globe, each trapped within the confines of this human-designed paradise. A Chinese red-crowned crane named Dao paced nervously nearby, her elegant wings clipped to prevent escape. Thoth, a hamadryas baboon from Egypt with a quick wit masked by his playful demeanor, swung from the monkey bars, a symbol of imprisoned exuberance. Blossom, a Monarch butterfly of breathtaking beauty, fluttered weakly, her delicate wings bearing the scars of glyphosate toxicity.

In the shared gaze of these imprisoned souls, Chi recognized the universal language of captivity—a silent plea for freedom that transcended species and borders.

Even in captivity, Chi retained the spirit of a king. Though confined to the confines of the theme park, his regal demeanor never wavered. He inspired hope among his fellow captives, urging them to hold onto their dignity and resilience in the face of adversity. In the distance, the rhythmic thud of construction echoed—a reminder that even in this seemingly idyllic place, the machinery of progress never ceased its relentless churn.

"We must find a way out," Chi stated one evening, his voice firm with resolve. The others gathered around, drawn by the strength of his presence.

"Aye, freedom is the song of our hearts," Dao replied, her voice as clear as the waters of her native rivers.

Thoth, tapping a branch rhythmically against the ground, added, "And cleverness our key. I've observed the guards; there's a pattern to their rounds."

Blossom fluttered above, her colors a whisper of hope. "And I've seen a gap in the fence, near the old oak. It's guarded, but not impossible to reach."

Their plan was daring, a testament to the indomitable spirit that thrived even in captivity. On the night of their escape, the park was alive with the sounds of a harvest festival. Music and laughter provided the perfect cover for their flight.

Chi led the charge, his hooves silent on the soft earth. Dao soared above, guiding them with her keen sight. Thoth provided a distraction, his antics drawing the attention of the guards away from the fence. Blossom, her flight a dance of light, marked the path to freedom.

As they breached the confines of their captivity, the world opened before them, vast and unknown. "To the wild," Chi whispered, his heart beating a rhythm of hope and fear. With a burst of strength and determination, he charged through the electrified service gate, his powerful limbs and long spiral horns smashing against the human-made barrier. The sound of splintering wood filled the air as Chi burst into the open, his heart pounding with a mix of exhilaration and fear. The sting of the voltage momentarily stunned him, but he quickly recovered his balance and forged on.

Together, the eclectic band of escapees embarked on a journey that would redefine the boundaries of their existence. Chi, once a captive in a foreign land, now led a motley crew of creatures bound by a common purpose—to remain free from the chains of human imposition and return to the wild realms they called home.

As the sun dipped below the horizon, casting long shadows across the Bay Area cityscape, Chi and his newfound companions disappeared into the cover of night. Their epic journey had just begun, and the challenges that lay ahead would test their resilience and forge bonds that transcended the boundaries of species and circumstance.

Little did they know that their quest for freedom would evolve into a larger-than-life odyssey—one that would weave through the tapestry of globalization, war, and climate change, and pit them against formidable foes and unexpected allies. Chiwara, Chi's namesake and the great semi-antelope deity of Mali, and Maat, the Egyptian goddess of truth and justice, watched over them from the celestial realms, their eyes reflecting the weight of the challenges that awaited.

As Chi and his companions ventured forth into the unknown, the moonlit savannah of West Africa seemed like a distant dream—a memory fading into the twilight of their shared destiny. The odyssey of Chi, king of the antelopes, had just begun, and the world awaited the epic tale that would unfold with every step they took on the long journey home.

2. The Escape

The night was their ally as Chi and his companions fled the theme park, their hooves, wings, and paws making hardly a sound against the soft soil. The scent of freedom hung in the air, mingling with the heady aroma of the California flora. Yet, as they made their way through the shadows, a palpable tension gripped the group.

Chi, his sinewy muscles tense with the thrill of escape, led the way. His regal presence, once confined to the stark boundaries of captivity, now emerged in full force. Dao, the red-crowned crane, soared gracefully overhead, her wings slicing through the cool night air. Thoth, the baboon with eyes that betrayed a keen intelligence, swung adeptly from branch to branch, his digital tablet clutched in his agile fingers. And Blossom, the Monarch butterfly, fluttered alongside, her delicate wings carrying her on the currents of the night.

The scent of freedom led them to an unlikely refuge—a produce wagon parked at the edge of the theme park. The

aroma of fresh fruits and vegetables wafted through the air, a stark contrast to the sterile captivity they had left behind. Without hesitation, they stealthily boarded the wagon, finding solace among the crates of organic produce.

As the wagon rumbled to life, Chi and his companions huddled together, their eyes reflecting a mix of relief and uncertainty. The journey had just begun, and the unfamiliar sights and sounds of the human world unfolded around them.

The truck's first stop was San Francisco, a city teeming with life and diversity. The Golden Gate Bridge loomed majestically in the distance, its iconic orange hue standing out against the night sky. The cable cars clanged and rattled through the streets, their tracks winding like serpents through the city.

"This place is so different from our homes," remarked Chi, gazing out at the bustling cityscape.

Dao, her elegant neck craning to take in the sights, nodded. "It's a world we never knew existed, and yet here we are."

Thoth, perched on a crate with his digital tablet in hand, couldn't resist chiming in. "Well, this city may be new to us, but the digital world is my domain. I'll keep an eye out for any electronic traces of our escape." He had learned computer skills at the theme park to the amusement of visitors, especially children, who took selfies with him.

As the wagon made its way to Fisherman's Wharf, the scent of saltwater and seafood filled the air. Seals barked in the distance, their playful antics a reminder of the natural world that existed beyond the concrete confines of the theme park.

Blossom, sipping nectar from a flower, observed, "Even in this bustling place, there's a beauty to be found."

Chi nodded, "Indeed, and beauty is what we must cherish as we journey forward."

Their next destination was the Presidio, where the historic military post stood silent in the moonlight. Thoth, engrossed in his tablet, mumbled, "No electronic traces yet. It seems we've eluded their digital grasp, at least for now."

As they wound through the narrow streets of Chinatown, lanterns swayed gently in the breeze, casting a warm glow over the cobblestone paths. Chi marveled at the resilience of the human spirit reflected in the vibrant colors and intricate designs.

Dao, her eyes sparkling with admiration, noted, "Creativity is not confined to the wild; humans have their own forms of expression."

As the wagon left the city lights behind, it ventured northward, leaving the urban landscape for the open expanse of the Sacramento Valley. The once cool night air turned heavy with the scent of agrochemicals—endless fields of fruits, nuts, and vegetables, sprayed with pesticides and grown with artificial fertilizers.

Thoth, squinting at his tablet, scowled. "The cyber jungle may be behind us, but these fields are a different kind of wilderness." He sampled some of the almonds and table grapes but spit them out because of their acrid, chemicalized taste.

Throughout their escape, Chi's leadership shone brightly, guiding the group through the perils of the human world with courage and wisdom. His determination to reclaim his freedom and reunite with his herd fueled their journey, driving them forward even in the darkest moments.

His eyes narrowed as he surveyed the vast expanses of cultivated land. "We must tread carefully; this is a perilous landscape."

The group trudged through the Sacramento Valley's vast monocultures of tomatoes, peaches, sunflowers, and alfalfa, their hooves and paws sinking into the soft soil. The air grew thick with the acrid scent of artificial fertilizer and pesticides, and Thoth's digital devices became an added weight—a constant reminder of the forces that sought to reclaim them.

As they navigated the challenges of this new world, their bond deepened, forged in the crucible of shared adversity. From the local wildlife, they learned of the region's shrinking habitat from urbanization, agriculture, and wildfires caused by climate change.

Along the way, they encountered Jasper, a coyote with tales of the land and advice for the travelers. "You're not the first to seek freedom in these parts," Jasper said one moonlit night, his eyes reflecting the firelight. "But you might be the first of your kind to make it."

"And we won't be the last," Chi vowed, his voice carrying the weight of his resolve.

A Chinook salmon named Silver told them, "We require constant flows to reproduce. The higher temperatures in recent years have forced many of us to move north." He related that unlike virtually all of his kind that travel the Sacramento River, his wife was able to lay eggs. "But the hatchlings died in the warmer waters, and she perished of a broken heart. I now will also migrate north to Canada and hope to find a new mate."

The animals wished the sorrowful salmon well in its long upstream journey.

Dao, her slender legs navigating the uneven terrain, spoke with determination. "We need a place to rest, away from these toxic fumes and waters. Somewhere pure, untouched by the hands of industry."

Thoth, his eyes scanning the horizon, nodded. "I'm on it. Let me find a sanctuary through the wonders of technology."

As they pressed on, Thoth tapped away on his tablet, searching for a refuge from the chemical-laden fields. It was then that Maat, the ancient Egyptian goddess of Truth, appeared in a spectral form, her eyes filled with an other-worldly wisdom.

"Follow the crane," she whispered, her voice echoing in the night. "Dao will guide you to a place where nature thrives, and human toxins cannot reach."

Emboldened by Maat's guidance, the group pressed forward, their eyes fixed on the crane soaring above. Through the moon-lit night, Dao led them to an unexpected haven—an organic rice farm nestled near the Feather River.

The farm was a sanctuary of biodiversity, where tiny fish swam in the paddy fields, frogs croaked in harmony, and insects hummed in a symphony of life. The air was pure, untainted by the chemicals that had clung to their fur, feathers, and wings.

Thoth, gazing around in awe, marveled, "This is a digital detox for the soul. I think we've found our safe haven."

Blossom was also ecstatic. Around the rice field she found patches of milkweed, the principal food of Monarch butterflies. Thanks to GMO Bt and glyphosate, its range had dramatically shrunk across the North American continent. What remained was often toxic, hence her own near-death experience.

For weeks, Chi and his companions reveled in the peace of the organic rice farm as the beautiful panicles of rice ripened. They bathed in the clear waters of the paddy fields, feasted on the abundance of grasses, buds, and fruit, and rested beneath the shade of ancient trees. The scars of captivity began to fade as the vibrant energy of the natural world healed their wounds.

As the days turned into weeks, Dao, Thoth, Blossom, and Chi

forged a bond that transcended the trials of their journey. In the quiet moments of reflection, they shared stories of their homelands, the challenges they faced, and the dreams that fueled their spirits.

One day, as Blossom fluttered among the flowers, her delicate wings catching the sunlight, she noticed a disturbance in the air. Thoth, his tablet in hand, furrowed his brow. "Someone is onto us. Electronic eyes are watching," he warned.

The idyllic respite of the organic rice farm was shattered by the ominous arrival of Robert Ott, the heartless scientist who had captured the leaping antelope, the resourceful baboon, and the keen-sighted crane. Wanted notices bearing the images of Chi and his companions circulated online, and the digital realm became a new battleground in their quest for freedom.

As the group gathered in urgency, Thoth devised a plan. "I'll use my digital skills to create false trails and confuse our pursuers. Meanwhile, we must be vigilant in the physical realm."

Blossom, hovering above the group, spoke with a sense of urgency. "I'll keep watch from above, searching for any signs of danger. The wind carries whispers, and I'll listen closely."

It was a delicate dance between the tangible and the digital, a dance that required both the ancient wisdom of Chiwara and Maat and the contemporary prowess of Thoth. As Chi and his companions braced themselves for the challenges ahead, the farm, once a sanctuary, became a battleground in the larger war for their freedom.

It was during one of Blossom's scouting missions that she sensed the imminent threat of capture. With delicate urgency, she fluttered back to the group, her wings carrying a warning. "Robert Ott is closing in. We must leave, now!"

The once tranquil fields of the organic rice farm were now filled with the urgency of impending danger. The group scrambled to gather their belongings, their eyes scanning the horizon for any sign of their relentless pursuer.

Just as the tension reached its peak, a rumbling sound filled the air—an old VW van, its engine sputtering and wheezing, emerged from the shadows. Behind the wheel sat Sophie Wood,

a local gardener and folksinger, who had sensed the plight of Chi and his companions after seeing an online wanted poster.

"Get in! We don't have much time!" she shouted, her eyes reflecting a fierce determination.

With a surge of gratitude, Chi and his companions piled into the old VW van, the doors closing just as Robert Ott's sinister silhouette appeared on the horizon. Sophie, her hands gripping the steering wheel with a steely resolve, navigated the winding roads, leaving the organic rice farm behind.

As the VW van rumbled into the night, Thoth leaned over to Chi and whispered, "Digital jungle, ancient wisdom, and a folksinger with a heart of gold — looks like we've got the perfect mix to outwit our pursuers."

With a nod from Chi, the group settled into the back of the VW wagon, their eyes fixed on the road ahead. The journey continued, the odyssey of Chi and his companions a testament to the indomitable spirit that bridged the realms of the natural and the digital, the ancient and the contemporary.

And so, under the moonlit sky, the unlikely band of fugitives ventured forth, their path unknown, their destination uncertain. In the words of Sophie, the folksinger who had become an unexpected ally, "Sometimes, the road to freedom is paved with melodies sung in the key of resilience, and the harmony of nature is our guide."

As the VW van carried them into the depths of the night, the echoes of their journey resonated — a symphony of tales unfolding, a testament to the power of unity, and the boundless spirit that compelled them to brave the challenges of a world in flux.

3. The Trek to the Desert Southwest

As they fled Northern California, Chi's role as king of the antelopes took on new significance. He became a beacon of hope for all creatures who longed for freedom, his strength and resilience inspiring others to stand against the forces of exploitation and oppression.

In the heart of the wilderness, Chi's leadership would be tested like never before, as he navigated the challenges of the natural world and confronted the harsh realities of human encroachment. But with the spirit of a king burning bright within him, Chi was prepared to face whatever trials lay ahead, for he knew that true kingship was not measured by power alone, but by the strength of character and compassion.

The old VW van rumbled along the desert roads, its tires kicking up dust in the wake of its journey. The fugitives — Chi the antelope, Dao the red-crowned crane, Thoth the baboon, and Blossom the Monarch butterfly — alongside their human ally, Sophie Wood, were on a quest for freedom that traversed the arid landscapes of the Southwest. The warmth of the sun pressed against the van's windows, casting shadows that danced along the walls of the confined space.

As they left the Sacramento Valley behind, the landscape transformed into vast stretches of desert, where the horizon seemed to stretch endlessly under the boundless sky. Sophie navigated the van through small towns and desert regions, avoiding the interstate to escape the prying eyes of law enforcement and a curious public that might mistake their unusual entourage for something more nefarious.

The journey was fraught with challenges, from encounters with the ever-watchful eyes of surveillance cameras to the relentless pursuit of law enforcement on the lookout for exotic animals. Thoth, ever the digital savant, constantly scanned the surroundings for electronic signals that might betray their presence.

"We must remain vigilant," warned Thoth. "The eyes of the digital world are everywhere, and we don't want to become unwitting stars on Instagram."

Dao, her elegant neck craned as she surveyed the desert expanse, nodded in agreement. "We are but fleeting guests in this human world. Our freedom depends on our ability to blend into the vastness of nature."

The van rumbled on, its engine carrying them through the silent expanses of the desert. As they approached northeastern Arizona, the terrain shifted, and mesas rose like ancient sentinels against the canvas of the sky.

Their destination, a Hopi village, was perched high atop one of these mesas, a place of refuge that Sophie had spoken of with a reverence that mirrored the respect she held for the land. The Hopi had a connection to the earth that transcended generations, a connection Chi and his companions longed to experience.

On the second day of their arduous journey, the van wound its way toward the Hopi village. The red earth beneath the wheels seemed to pulse with ancient energy, and the air carried the scent of sage and cedar. As they approached, the mesa loomed in the distance—a fortress of rock and earth, etched with the echoes of a civilization that had endured for centuries.

Upon arrival, Sophie's friends from the Hopi village welcomed them with open arms. The villagers, with weathered faces and eyes that held the wisdom of the ages, greeted the animals and their human companion with a quiet respect. The Hopi knew the struggles of the land, the challenges faced by both humans and animals in the wake of modernity's relentless advance.

In the heart of the village, the *kiva* awaited—a large, circular, underground room that seemed to breathe with the rhythms of the earth. It became the temporary sanctuary for Chi and his companions, a place where the walls whispered tales of resilience and survival.

In the village, they encountered other animals, each with a story etched into the tapestry of the land. Crown, the bald eagle, perched majestically on a rocky outcrop, his keen eyes surveying the horizon. Drizzle, the bear, meandered through the village, her fur a testament to the wildness that still lingered in the heart of the mesa. Howl, the wolf, moved with a silent grace, his presence a reminder of the spirits that roamed the vastness of the Southwest. Slither, the rattlesnake, slinked through the shadows, a creature of both fear and reverence.

Under the vast desert sky, Chi and his companions gathered with these indigenous inhabitants, sharing stories of the perils faced since the Manhattan Project in Los Alamos, uranium mining, and the contamination of water and soil. The Hopi and Navajo people recounted epidemics of cancer and other diseases, not only among themselves but also among the wild and domestic animals that roamed the once pristine landscapes.

"Howl, have you seen the changes in the land over the years?" Chi inquired, his eyes reflecting a deep concern.

Howl, his gaze fixed on the distant horizon, replied with a mournful howl that seemed to carry the weight of generations. "The spirits of the land weep for what has been lost. The rivers no longer sing the songs of abundance, and the earth is scarred by the insatiable hunger of progress."

Crown, his wings casting a shadow over the gathering, added, "The skies, once pure and untainted, bear witness to the consequences of human folly. The winds now carry the whispers of despair."

As the animals and humans shared their tales, the desert sun dipped below the horizon, casting hues of orange and pink across the vast expanse. The villagers invited Chi and his companions to partake in a Hopi Buffalo Dance, a sacred ritual that celebrated the connection between humans, animals, and the earth.

The drumbeat echoed through the night, guiding the dancers in rhythmic movements that mirrored the heartbeat of the land. Chi and his companions, drawn into the dance, felt the pulse of the desert beneath their hooves, wings, and paws. Sophie, too, joined the dance, her steps interwoven with the ancient traditions of the Hopi.

Amidst the dance, a great buffalo emerged—a majestic being named Thunder. His massive form moved with a grace that belied his size, and his eyes held a wisdom that transcended the confines of his earthly existence.

As the dance continued, a mystical experience unfolded. Maat, the ancient Egyptian goddess of Truth, and Chiwara, the African antelope-headed deity appeared alongside Native American spiritual guardians, their ethereal presence weaving through the rhythmic dance. Chi and his companions felt a surge of inspiration, a cosmic connection that bound them to the ancient spirits and the land they traversed.

The dance continued into the night, the drumbeat echoing across the mesa like a heartbeat that resonated through the ages. In that sacred moment, the boundaries between species, cultures, and realms seemed to dissolve, and the desert became a canvas upon which the spirits painted tales of resilience and hope.

As the festivities reached their zenith, a sudden disruption shattered the serenity—a surveillance drone swooped down from the sky over the mesa. The villagers, recognizing the intrusion, exchanged uneasy glances. The animals, sensing the imminent threat, gathered in hushed urgency.

"We've been identified," Thoth muttered, his eyes fixed on the mechanical intruder.

The crane Dao, her majestic wings unfurled, spoke with a sense of urgency. "The eyes of the sky are upon us. We must leave at first light, or our sanctuary will become a battleground."

The revelry faded, replaced by a solemn acknowledgment of the challenges that lay ahead. The villagers, understanding the precariousness of Chi and his companions, offered words of encouragement and a blessing for their journey.

As the night wore on, Chi and his companions found themselves once again huddled in the kiva, the underground room that had become a refuge from the storms of the human world. The desert winds whispered tales of ancient spirits, and the flickering torchlight cast shadows that danced upon the earthen walls.

In the quiet of the night, Dao spoke with a wisdom that transcended language. "Our journey is not just about reclaiming freedom; it is about forging alliances with the spirits of the land, both ancient and contemporary."

4. The Flight of the Monarchs

The VW van rolled along dusty roads, crossing the border into Mexico with a mixture of trepidation and relief. Sophie, behind the wheel, joked, "Most immigrants are heading the other way," a light-hearted comment that belied the weight of their journey. The open road stretched ahead, a vast expanse of possibility and uncertainty.

Blossom, the Monarch butterfly, suggested they head for the Oyamel fir forests just west of Mexico City, her ancestral home. "The Monarch butterfly sanctuary is a place of refuge. We'll blend in with the orange and black clouds of my kin returning for the Dia de los Muertos — Day of the Dead — celebration."

The VW van traversed the southern landscapes, accompanied by the hum of the engine and the rhythmic beat of its tires on the well-worn road. Along the way, they encountered *compesinos* — local farmers who welcomed them with open arms and shared the bounty of their harvest. Tortillas, beans, and squash — the Three Sisters — formed the basis of the native foodways, a reminder of the deep connection between people and the land.

As they dined under the shade of a gnarled tree, a compesino named Carlos spoke of the Aztec emperor's addiction and cravings. "The emperor and his court believed Xocolatl (chocolate) had divine properties, and its use in funeral rituals and war contributed to their delusional world-view, one that demanded human sacrifice to keep the cosmos in balance."

Thoth, engrossed in the conversation, jotted down notes on his tablet. "The extreme diet of the Aztecs, including snakes and reptiles, further fueled the cult of sacrifice and violence. It's a testament to how deeply intertwined food, culture, and belief systems can be."

Dao, the red-crowned crane, listened intently, her elegant form poised in quiet contemplation. "Food reflects society's values. The Aztecs' extreme dietary preferences had far-reaching consequences for their people and the land."

The journey continued, the VW van weaving through the tapestry of Mexico's diverse landscapes. Dao, during a brief rest stop, encountered a condor named Profunda, perched on a rocky outcrop. Profunda lamented the introduction of GMO corn forced upon Mexicans by NAFTA. Thoth, eager to contribute his digital wisdom, offered advice drawn from the ancient culture of Egypt.

"Genetic engineering and the use of pesticides threaten the native maizefields of Mexico. The Mayans revered maize, and its endangerment is a challenge that resonates with cultures across time and space."

As they moved southward, Chi encountered Great Horn, a Mexican pronghorn antelope, whose species faced endangerment due to habitat destruction, overgrazing, and poaching. Great Horn shared his plight with empathy for the refugees, observing, "My horn is prized as an aphrodisiac, and we constantly have to evade poachers and their sensors and traps."

The VW van pressed on, navigating the rugged terrain until the Oyamel fir forests came into view. The air, scented with the freshness of pine, carried a promise of sanctuary. Sophie parked the van at the edge of the forest, and the group, accompanied by Blossom, ventured deeper into the woodland.

As they entered the realm of the Monarchs, a breathtaking sight unfolded—a vast cloud of orange and black butterflies with bright white spots, returning from their annual thousands-mile migration across North America. Blossom's kin, resplendent in their delicate beauty, filled the air with a fluttering symphony.

The Monarchs were returning for the Dia de los Muertos celebration, honoring the spirits of loved ones who had passed away. Roosting in fir trees up to 2 miles above sea level, they transformed the forest into a living tapestry of vibrant color. In addition to GMOs, the beautiful butterflies and other insects and birds were dying from exposure to cell towers, power lines, giant windmills, and other smart infrastructure that caused them to lose their sense of direction and natural immunity to disease.

Chi and his companions, welcomed by the butterfly elders, joined the festivities. The air resonated with the soft rustle of wings, the laughter of creatures from all corners of the woodland, and the scent of pine mingled with the aroma of marigolds—a flower believed to guide the spirits back to the world of the living.

As the night deepened, a vision unfolded. Quetzacoatl, the Feathered Serpent of Mexica myth, appeared before Chi and his companions. His majestic form, a blend of vibrant colors, seemed to embody the very essence of the natural world.

"The decline of the Monarchs, major pollinators, is affecting the balance of the natural environment," lamented Quetzacoatl. "Wild animals naturally sequester carbon when they burrow or make their nests. Dwindling numbers and loss of their habitat is driving global warming," he continued.

"Blossom, Chi, Thoth, Dao, and Sophie, your quest is intertwined with the fate of the land. Continue your journey with purpose and understanding."

In the mystical glow of the Dia de los Muertos celebration, the air shimmered with ancestral wisdom and cosmic guidance. Maat, the ancient Egyptian goddess of Truth, wove a dreamy spell over the gathering, casting a veil of tranquility and insight.

As dawn approached, the refugees, now a part of the butterfly celebration, felt the rhythmic beat of wings as the Monarchs prepared to cluster together for warmth, conserving energy until the arrival of spring. The air was filled with a sense of unity, a connection between the ancient and the contemporary, the winged and the hoofed.

The butterfly elders, their wings gently folded, extended an invitation to the newcomers. "Rest among us, for the night is long, and the dreams of Dia de los Muertos carry messages from the ancestors. In your slumber, seek the guidance that will propel you toward the next destination in your journey."

And so, under the watchful gaze of the Monarchs and the cosmic energies that infused the Oyamel fir forest, Chi and his companions fell into a deep, well-needed slumber. The dreamscape unfolded, carrying them into the realms of ancient spirits, modern challenges, and the promise of a world yet to be discovered. The journey of Chi, Dao, Thoth, Blossom, and Sophie continued, guided by the wisdom of the land, the spirits, and the cosmic forces that wove their destiny across the vast tapestry of existence.

5. The Whispering Stones

The Oyamel fir mountains stood tall and proud, their peaks crowned with a mantle of ancient wisdom and the vibrant hues of the Monarch butterflies. As dawn painted the sky in hues of pink and gold, Chi and his companions gathered to bid farewell to Blossom and Sophie.

The air was filled with a bittersweet melody as Blossom, her wings folded delicately, addressed the group. "I must stay here to recuperate over the winter. This sanctuary has been my home, and the flutter of Monarch wings my lullaby. Carry the spirit of the butterflies with you on your journey."

Tears glistened in Chi's eyes as he nuzzled Blossom, understanding the sacrifice she made for their freedom. Sophie, too, stood beside the VW van, her gaze fixed on the three remaining refugees. "This old van can't navigate the jungles or deserts that lie ahead. I'm heading back to Northern California, but you carry a piece of my heart with you."

With a final embrace and a promise to reunite, the travelers parted ways. Blossom and Sophie remained in the embrace of the Oyamel fir mountains, while Chi, Dao, and Thoth followed a gorgeous quetzal bird that emerged from the depths of the forest. The resplendent creature led them through the Yucatan, where they slipped unnoticed into a flock of sheep, horses, aardvarks, and other animals bound for South America on a ship traversing the Gulf of Mexico.

In Bolivia, the landscape shifted once again as they found themselves on the world's largest salt flat—the Salar de Uyuni. The vast expanse, also known as the Lithium Triangle, held 60% of the world's lithium reserves, extracted for batteries that powered electric vehicles, cell phones, and other electronic devices.

As twilight descended, the trio traipsed through the jungle on the outskirts of the salt flats. In the dense foliage, Chi thrust aside large ferns with his majestic horns and marveled at the diversity of wildlife. "The spirits of the jungle are vibrant and alive. Every rustle and chirp tell a tale."

A sudden rustle in the undergrowth signaled danger. Lithe, a jaguar with sleek, spotted fur, pounced on Chi with deadly intent. The air crackled with tension as fur flew and feathers fell.

In the chaos, Dao, with her long sharp beak, and Thoth, wielding the menacing stylus from his tablet like a spear, intervened with lightning speed. As the jungle echoed with the sounds of the struggle, Squeeze, a great anaconda, fell between them from a tree in which she was coiled. Squeeze, her coils separating the two sides, commanded Lithe to halt.

"The spirits protect these newcomers. They are not to be harmed," declared Squeeze, her emerald eyes fixed on the jaguar.

Lithe, his demeanor transformed, bowed his head in submission. "I did not recognize their protected status. I am at your service, honored guests."

Chi and his companions, their hearts still pounding from the

encounter, relaxed. Lithe, his spotted coat shimmering in the dappled moonlight, now spoke of the environmental devastation caused by the lithium mines. "The health of the jungle is intertwined with the balance of its inhabitants. The Lithium mines are poisoning the air, soil, and water, causing devastation that ripples through nature."

"The colossal amount of water used in lithium mining has caused draught, devastating the local flora and fauna," Lithe continued shaking his long whiskers. Indicating ponds in the distance that ranged in color from a pinky white to a turquoise and a highly concentrated, canary yellow, Lithe recalled sadly that his mate Sinowy and cubs had died of drinking toxic water. "I can no longer survive in such an environment," he lamented. He further observed that because of warmer temperatures, many animals in the region had also migrated to higher elevations. "May I join you in your travels?" Lithe asked humbly.

Chi, Dao, and Thoth were delighted to welcome the muscular jaguar as the new fourth member of their troupe. Lithe purred blissfully like a kitten at their acceptance.

The journey continued to Norte Chico in northern Peru, the site of the earliest civilization in South America. The ruins of ancient pyramids bore witness to the ingenuity of early human societies. Dolly, a matronly llama, welcomed the group, sharing tales of a time when humanity embraced peace and kindness.

Dao, with her elegant neck and red crown, spoke up: "Tell us of the ancient history of this land, Dolly. The pathways and stones speak of a rich heritage, and I yearn to understand more." The shaggy llama, her eyes reflecting the wisdom of the Andean mountains, began weaving tales of ancient South American civilizations. "The first culture at Norte Chico were pioneers in agriculture, cultivating a variety of crops, including the sacred quinoa. The Incans, later on, expanded these practices, creating a network of terraced fields that embraced the contours of the land and benefited four- and two-legged alike."

"Metallurgy was another marvel," the llama continued. "Gold, silver, copper, and emerald were crafted into intricate ornaments and tools. The original human inhabitants, with their skilled hands, shaped a world where artistry and utility coexisted. They made beautiful ribbons, bonnets, and bells for the animals and shared their quinoa, potatoes, and other food in times of drought and hunger."

Thoth, intrigued by the mention of tools, chimed in, "What of the quipu, these knotted strings you speak of? How were they used in Andean societies?"

Dolly explained, "The quipu was an ingenious system of record-keeping and communication. Different knots, colors, and positions conveyed numerical and categorical information. It was a language of strings, a bridge between the tangible and the abstract. They also recorded many songs and stories about animal emissaries and spirits."

Chi, pondering the vibrant history, asked, "And what of the fabric bridges that are now whispers in the wind?"

Dolly's eyes lit up with passion. "The Andeans built fabric suspension bridges, called *q'eswachaka*, that spanned impassable chasms. They were woven from ichu grass and fibers from llamas and alpacas, strong and resilient. They enabled animals as well as humans to travel efficiently from place to place without long, potentially hazardous detours. It was a time when mutual harmony between the human and animal realm prevailed."

"What about the massive stone complexes?" Chi further inquired.

"They were not just structures," the llama replied. "They were celestial observatories, granaries, and shrines. The stones whispered the secrets of a civilization lost to time.

"In a later era, the Incan Empire arose, bringing with it exploitation, conscription, and human and animal sacrifice," Dolly continued.

"But not all of Incan history is cruel. Let me take you to Aramu Muru, the 'Gate of the Gods,' where legend speaks of a golden disk dropped from the sky."

At Aramu Muru, the travelers marveled at the massive stone carving. Dao, her beak tracing the intricate carvings, whispered, "The stones resonate with ancient energies. The spirits of this place speak to us."

As they stood on one of the high Andean summits, the air tingling with cosmic energy, Chiwara and Maat, assisted by local spirits, sent a collective vision—a door opening, bathed in golden light. A sense of unity and purpose enveloped the travelers, transcending time and space. In awe, Dolly presented Thoth with a multicolored quipu, "Its cord is made from my hair. May it help guide you in your journey."

Unbeknownst to them, high above, a surveillance satellite captured their likenesses and identified Chi, Thoth, and their companions. The authorities were alerted to their location, setting the stage for the next chapter in their odyssey.

6. Echoes of the Past

The Andes, cloaked in verdant green, gradually surrendered their towering peaks to the lush embrace of the great Amazon rainforest. As the party descended through the dense foliage, the air thick with humidity, a sense of being watched hung in the atmosphere. They couldn't see the satellites, but an instinctual awareness prickled their senses.

In this vibrant jungle, the air buzzed with the calls of unseen creatures — sloths lounging in the treetops, toucans with vibrant beaks, and poison dart frogs adding pops of color to the undergrowth. Thoth, the baboon with a penchant for technology, found a kindred spirit in a black spider monkey named Streak.

Streak swung gracefully from branch to branch, guiding the travelers through towering canopies, giant ferns, and twisting vines. Thoth marveled at the seemingly untouched wilderness, and Streak, with a knowing look, shared a different perspective. "Appearances can be deceiving. Millennia ago, sprawling human structures and sophisticated cultures thrived in Llanos de Mojos, and this region held the fabled City of Gold sought by Spanish explorers."

Dao, the red-crowned crane, descended from her aerial scouting to join the conversation. "I've seen immense figures etched into the earth, reminiscent of the Nazca lines in southern Peru."

Streak confirmed her observations. "Those are geoglyphs, remnants of a time when unity prevailed among the plant, animal, and human kingdoms. Llano de Mojos was once adorned with vast platforms, pyramid architecture, raised causeways, and extensive reservoirs and canals."

Dao nodded, her elegant neck swaying gracefully. "These lands tell stories that time itself has almost forgotten."

Moving deeper into the jungle, the party encountered Honeycomb, a member of the Casarabe indigenous community. Her eyes reflected the rich tapestry of her ancestry. "My people farmed maize and lived in harmony with the totem animals, honoring a covenant that celebrated the interconnectedness of all life."

As Honeycomb sang a heartfelt song about the oneness of creation, her voice resonated through the rain forest. In her headband, her listeners, both animal and human, felt the ethereal touch of Maat's feather, a symbol of justice and balance.

Lithe, the once-menacing jaguar, remarked on the fertile black soil beneath their feet. Honeycomb explained that it was *terra preta*, a product of weathered charcoal mixed with compost, manure, pottery, and bones—a sustainable farming technique practiced by indigenous communities for thousands of years.

"Like many native communities, we face decline and displacement," Honeycomb shared, her eyes reflecting the struggle. "Logging, mining, and monocultures are eroding the heart of the rainforest. Terra preta, a testament to our ancestral wisdom, holds the promise of regeneration."

As the sun dipped below the horizon, painting the sky in hues of crimson and gold, Chi and his companions found themselves immersed in the heart of the Amazon rainforest. The air was thick with the scent of lush vegetation, and the sounds of the forest echoed all around them—a symphony of chirping insects, rustling leaves, and distant calls of unseen creatures.

Amidst the towering trees and tangled undergrowth, Honeycomb led them to a hidden village, nestled within a clearing adorned with colorful blooms and winding vines. The village was a testament to the ancient Amazonian culture, a civilization that had thrived in harmony with the natural world for centuries.

The buildings, constructed from woven palm leaves and sturdy vines, blended seamlessly with the surrounding jungle, their curved roofs reaching toward the canopy above. Around the village, gardens teeming with exotic fruits and vegetables flourished under the dappled sunlight, tended to by villagers who moved with the grace and agility of the creatures with whom they shared their home.

Chi and his companions were greeted warmly by the villagers, who welcomed them with open arms and curious glances. They marveled at the sight of the strange travelers—Chi with his regal bearing, Thoth with his wise eyes and knowing smile, Dao with her red plume, and Lithe with dreamy eyes and purr of a kitten.

As they wandered through the village, Chi and his companions learned more about the ancient Amazonian culture and its sustainable practices. They listened to stories of how the villagers lived in harmony with the land, using traditional methods of farming and hunting that respected the delicate balance of nature.

"These lands have been our home for generations," explained one of the villagers, a wise elder with weathered skin and eyes that sparkled with ancient wisdom. "We have learned to live in harmony with the forest, taking only what we need and giving back to the earth in return. It is a way of life that has sustained us for centuries."

As they listened to the elder's words, Chi and his companions felt a deep sense of reverence for the ancient Amazonian culture and its profound connection to the natural world. They realized that in their quest to unite the animals of the world, they must also strive to protect the habitats and ecosystems that sustained them all.

As the travelers continued their journey, they reached a human outpost on a tributary of the mighty Amazonian waterway. The floating houseboat harbored a small store where Thoth needed to replace the dwindling battery in his tablet. Despite the conflict of using lithium, the necessity for self-defense prevailed.

"I must apologize, Lithe," Thoth confessed, "for relying on a lithium battery and harmful artificial electromagnetic radiation. But this device can help detect drones and avoid capture."

Lithe acknowledged the necessity of desperate measures in desperate times. He admitted to chewing through cell tower cables to block EMFs and preserve wildlife. He offered to create a distraction while Thoth sneaked inside the small outpost to procure a new battery. Lithe, with a burst of energy, created chaos outside, drawing attention of the people within.

However, as Thoth entered the floating outpost, he found himself face-to-face with an unexpected adversary—Robert Ott, the relentless bounty hunter from California.

"Thoth, you wily baboon, come with me," Ott growled, his voice dripping with menace as he seized the unsuspecting baboon by the arm. "You're coming with me, like it or not."

Thoth struggled against Ott's grasp, his eyes flashing with anger and defiance. "Let me go, you brute!" he snarled, his voice rising above the din of the rapidly flowing river.

But Ott was relentless, his grip like iron as he dragged Thoth away. With a cunning glint in his eyes, he dropped a net over Thoth and bundled him into a waiting speedboat. The small craft sped away, cutting through the murky waters of the Amazon tributary. The remaining animals, their faces etched with shock and helplessness, watched as Thoth was carried away from their midst, leaving them to ponder their destiny.

As Ott disappeared into the shadows of the forest, Chi and his companions knew that their journey had taken a dangerous turn. With Thoth in the clutches of their enemy, they must now embark on a daring rescue mission to save their friend and ensure that justice prevailed.

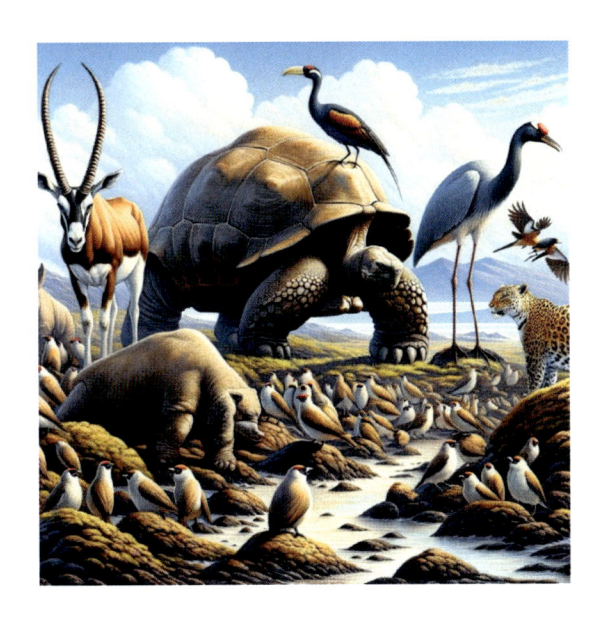

7. Songs of Freedom

Dao, the red-crowned crane, soared above, her keen eyes tracking the path of the motorboat carrying Robert Ott and the abducted Thoth. Several hours after the boat disappeared into the distance, Dao returned and spiraled down to rejoin Chi and Lithe. Her elegant form landed on the rocky terrain, and she delivered the news with a solemn tone.

"They are heading toward a port in Ecuador," Dao reported breathlessly. "I overheard a crewman saying that Thoth will be transferred to a scientific research vessel bound for the Galapagos Islands to undergo CRISPR gene editing."

Chi, his eyes reflecting determination, nodded. "We need to reach the Pacific coast and find a way to the Galapagos. Time is of the essence."

"I'll keep tracking the motorboat while you make your way to the Pacific coast," Dao informed them. "I'll circle back every few days to monitor your progress and keep in touch."

The dense humidity of the Pacific coast enveloped Chi and Lithe as they made their way toward the port in Ecuador. The jaguar moved with sinuous grace, his powerful muscles propelling him through the tangled underbrush. Chi, with his majestic horns lowered, navigated the dense foliage with an elegance born of survival.

After the return journey across the Andes, the duo finally reached the Pacific coast, a vast expanse of azure meeting golden shores. The shimmering waves beckoned, and they embarked on a quest to find passage to the Galapagos.

In the port, they encountered a bustling scene of fishermen mending nets, locals selling vibrant fruits, and ships of various sizes bobbing in the harbor. A weathered sailor, intrigued by the unconventional pair of a jaguar and an antelope, spoke out.

"Need passage to the Galapagos, eh? Well, I reckon I've got room on the *Midnight Mariner*. She's a sturdy vessel, weathered many a storm."

Gratitude glimmered in Chi's eyes as they boarded the *Midnight Mariner*, their gateway to the isolated haven of the Galapagos. The salty breeze whispered tales of ancient seas, and the anticipation of reuniting with Dao and rescuing Thoth hung thick in the air.

A few days later, the Galapagos Islands emerged on the horizon, a surreal collection of volcanic landscapes and teeming wildlife. The *Midnight Mariner* glided into a quiet bay.

Dao joined them on the shore, her bright crimson and yellow wings catching the sunlight. "The research vessel is there," she pointed. "We need to approach with caution and gather allies among the island's inhabitants."

In the Galapagos, the trio surveyed the serene beauty of the islands. *The Observer*, a scientific research vessel, lay anchored in a bay. Determined to rescue Thoth, they enlisted the support of the island's inhabitants, both feathered and scaled.

The trio set off on the rocky terrain, encountering curious blue-footed boobies, playful sea lions, and the iconic giant tortoises that roamed freely. Their journey led them to a poingnant setting—a gathering of animals, both ancient and wise.

Gargantua, the two-hundred-something-year-old tortoise, stood as a testament to the enduring spirit of the islands. His wrinkled eyes reflected centuries of observation, and his ancient voice resonated with tales of survival.

"I encountered young Charles Darwin when I was a mere hatchling," Gargantua began, his words carrying the weight of history. "He stalked many of my kith and kin, including my father, for turtle soup. It was a dish coveted by the British Navy and its naturalists."

Thoth, intrigued by the tortoise's wisdom, couldn't resist injecting a touch of humor. "From a 'you-are-what-you-eat' perspective, that might explain why Darwin was so slow and lethargic in developing the doctrine of evolution."

"No offense intended," he hastily added.

"None taken," the long-lived tortoise smiled. "Oft times, slowness is a virtue."

Beak, an elder finch with vibrant plumage, added her voice to the conversation. "Darwin also took my ancestors back to Europe. He carried a shotgun everywhere, collecting specimens without respecting their lives, families, and innate vitality."

The group engaged in a poignant discussion about the harrowing nature of scientific and medical research. Gargantua's observation resonated with the shared experiences of beings who had witnessed the evolving face of exploration. They recalled Thoth telling of grisly medical experiments involving implanted electrodes and testing with toxic cosmetics.

Days passed in the tranquil embrace of the Galapagos, the quartet forging alliances with the island's inhabitants. They conversed with sea lions lounging on sunlit rocks, sought counsel from wise old tortoises, and danced with the rhythm of blue-footed boobies. Each encounter added a layer to their understanding of the delicate balance between nature and the relentless pursuit of knowledge.

As they strolled through the island's diverse landscapes, Dao spotted *The Observer* anchored in a secluded bay. The trio, now accompanied by a growing assembly of allies, prepared to rescue Thoth.

Later that day, the sea around the Galapagos stirred with

unusual activity as a gigantic oceanic manta ray known as Stunning surfaced. The majestic creature, a symbol of the ocean's fragility, drew the attention of scientists eager to capture it for study or, in darker circles, for profit on the black market.

A flock of fierce birds, including brown pelicans, heron gulls, Nazca boobies, the Eurasian whimbrel, and numerous finches, descended upon the research vessel. Dive bombings and sharp beaks wreaked havoc, forcing the researchers into the deep.

"We sure upended those traffickers," Magenta, a scarlet flycatcher, boasted proudly after the encounter.

Lithe, with his sleek fur blending into the shadows, stealthily approached the research ship. The creaking sound of the gangway against the hull masked his movements as he infiltrated *The Observer*. Thoth, confined in a cage, greeted Lithe with eyes that sparkled with intelligence and resilience.

The jaguar's powerful limbs and sharp teeth made short work of the cage, and they swiftly exited the vessel. The human receptionist, frozen in fear by the intimidating presence of Chi's lowered long pointed horns, remained pinned to her desk. Thoth, seizing the opportunity, grabbed his confiscated tablet — a valuable tool for their journey — and threw the vials of his DNA overboard.

The trio escaped to an uninhabited part of the island chain, seeking refuge on a great outcropping where a long feather lay — a symbol of the finches, their terrestrial protectors, and Maat and Chiwara, their heavenly guardians of truth.

As they gathered under the vast sky, the ancient islands bearing witness to their tales, the wind carried whispers of freedom. In the embrace of nature's sanctuary, Chi, Lithe, and Thoth knew that their journey was far from over.

8. Voices of the Ocean

The vast expanse of the Pacific Ocean stretched before them, an endless canvas of blue meeting the sky in an unbroken horizon. The travelers, now aboard the native catamaran stocked with provisions, set sail due west from the Galapagos Islands. The rhythm of the ocean became their constant companion, and a group of giant tortoises bid them farewell, their ancient eyes reflecting the wisdom of millennia.

As the catamaran glided over the undulating waves, Dao, the red-crowned crane, maintained her surveillance from above. Her keen eyes scanned the ocean, and she reported back to Chi and Lithe on the researcher's island-wide search following Thoth's escape.

"Stay vigilant," she urged. "They are determined to find him, but we have the vastness of the ocean on our side."

The weeks at sea unfolded in a tranquil dance with nature. The catamaran made steady progress, and the travelers struck up conversations with a variety of marine life. Against the backdrop of the boundless ocean, the creatures shared their hopes and dreams.

Chi, his eyes reflecting the vast savannahs of West Africa, spoke of his longing to return to his kingdom. "We roamed freely, racing through stands of wild rice and millet, nibbling as we went. The Niger River was a source of endless fascination, and the people carved beautiful statues and fashioned elegant jewelry and headdresses of antelopes for celebrations."

Dao, her memories soaring over the Yellow River plain in North China, expressed a desire to reunite with her mate Lao. They had been separated when traffickers abducted her for her feathers, which fetched a princely sum on the fashion industry black market. "I yearn to find her and return to our nest."

Thoth, the resourceful baboon, shared the pain of being separated from his family in upper Egypt near the Nile. "I was captured while hunting for nuts and berries. Tranquilized and taken to a DNA research facility in America, I yearn for the day I can return to Kemet, the Black Land, as it was once known."

Lithe, the jaguar, lamented the toxic wasteland that once was his home. "Now, I seek a new place to call home and put down roots, to have a new family and live free."

As the travelers reflected on their pasts and dreamed of futures, a monster typhoon suddenly arose, casting their little catamaran into chaos. The raging storm tossed them into the briny deep, and survival became their sole focus as they clung to debris.

Amid the tempest, a giant Pacific octopus named Clutch emerged, her shiny black head and numerous arms providing a lifeline to the struggling creatures. The typhoon's wrath surrounded them, but Clutch's strength and determination propelled them away from the storm's heart.

Apologizing for her weakened state due to the infiltration of microplastics in the oceans, Clutch assured them of their safety. As the storm abated, the octopus guided them toward a small ship named *The Eyewitness*, the newest addition to the Ocean Shepherd fleet.

The Eyewitness was a vessel committed to environmental causes. With solar panels, wind turbines, and an optimized power management system, it stood as a beacon for ocean conservation. Clutch, in her aquatic grace, explained how *The*

Eyewitness had intervened against deep-sea mining and protested the release of radioactive water from Fukushima that was poisoning the deep.

Aboard the ship, the wet and hungry survivors found an unexpected sanctuary. Jomo Moussa, the seasoned captain, a native of Kenya, greeted them with a warm smile. "We're vegans on this vessel," he remarked, to which Lithe, the jaguar, surprised the humans by indicating his newly acquired preference for leafy greens, mushrooms, and wild grains.

When Jomo expressed skepticism that carnivores ate cereals, Lithe explained that prehistoric Argentina had the world's only fox that was ever tamed by humans. "I once met a foxy lady fox in Cañada Seca who ate the same proportion of maize as the people with whom she lived in harmony." He went on to add, "Like some of the birds in my region I would collect kernels of maize, drop them on hot rocks, and enjoy popcorn."

The Eyewitness, having just returned from protesting off coastal Japan, now planned to head to Australia. As the drenched and tired survivors settled in for the journey, Clutch, their eight-limbed savior, transformed herself into the form of an Ankh — an ancient Egyptian symbol of life.

Bidding farewell to their new underwater companion, the travelers marveled at the twists of fate that had brought them to *The Eyewitness*. Once again, the goddess Maat, the embodiment of truth, had intervened, guiding them through the perils of the storm to a vessel dedicated to preserving the life within the oceans. The South Seas, vast and unfathomable, now cradled them on their continuing journey toward the unknown.

49

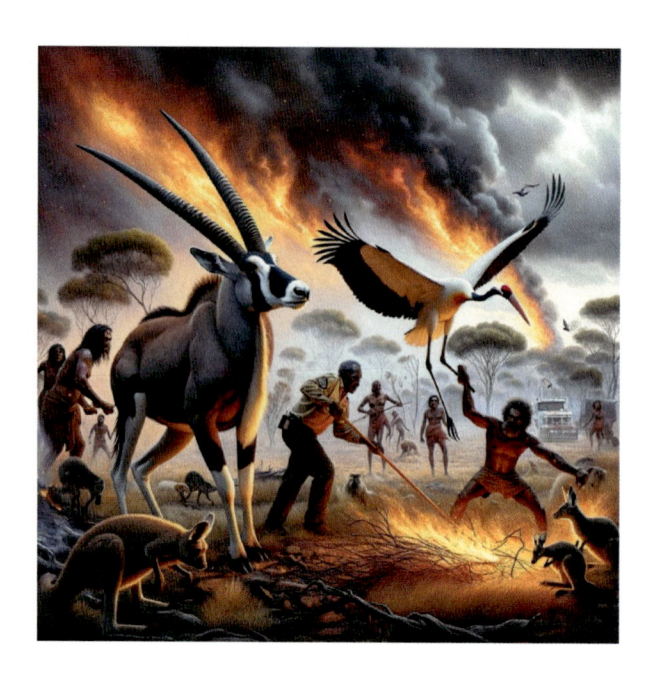

9. Fire Dance Down Under

The Eyewitness anchored in the port city of Darwin, embraced by the Northern Territory's coastal beauty. Nestled at the doorstep of the Outback, Darwin was a mosaic of modernity and the ancient land. Chi, Dao, Thoth, and Lithe disembarked, eager to explore the city's vibrant culture and delve into the heart of Australia.

Darwin sprawled along the Timor Sea, a city where skyscrapers shared the skyline with the ancient Kakadu escarpment. The air resonated with the scents of saltwater, eucalyptus, and the earthy undertones of the Outback. A diverse community thrived in this tropical haven, with one of the largest concentrations of ancestral aborigines.

The quartet found themselves transported in an organic farm truck, winding through the vast interior of the Northern Territory. Eventually, they arrived at a native community where people, descendants of the first settlers over 60,000 years ago, welcomed them with open arms.

The aboriginal customs unfolded before Chi and his companions, revealing a tapestry of traditions and beliefs that had weathered the eons. The community's daily sustenance was drawn from wild grains and predominantly plant-based foods, a harmonious dance with the land that had sustained them for generations.

Delighted by the telepathic connection among the aborigines, Dao remarked, "They are like birds and animals in that respect. Of course, we cranes use song and dance to emphasize certain feelings, but usual communication is shared just by thinking."

Nunkeri, a bouncy jill or young female kangaroo whose name meant "beautiful," became an instant friend. Thoth's flirtatious banter and his penchant for placing his new computer tablet in Nunkeri's pouch brought lightheartedness to the group. "Your pouch is like a cozy little mobile home," Thoth teased, causing Nunkeri to hop playfully in response.

As summer reached its zenith in the Southern Hemisphere, an ominous threat loomed over the landscape—a colossal wildfire that raged across the Australian terrain. The government, grappling with the inadequacy of modern firefighting methods, turned to the aboriginals for guidance, tapping into a legacy of selective fire management that spanned millennia.

Nunkeri explained the chronic wildfires fueled by industrialization, agriculture, and mining. "My parents and siblings perished in the conflagrations," she lamented. The animals joined forces with the aboriginals, embarking on a heroic effort to control the fire. "They occasionally eat birds and animals, but only what is necessary to survive," she added. "Today, factory farms, medical research, and the fashion industry wantonly take the lives of countless species."

Dao, holding lit twigs in her mouth, dropped them strategically to ignite counterfires, limiting the main inferno's advance. Chi, Thoth, and Lithe worked alongside the community, creating fire breaks and moving brush. The aboriginals employed a circular strategy, a dance of flames that mirrored the ancient spirallic patterns they used to sculpt the landscape.

After a valiant effort that left Dao's tail feathers singed, the collective force of Aboriginals and animals succeeded. The fire was halted just before it encroached on the outskirts of Darwin.

The community, along with their unlikely animal heroes, became celebrated across the nation, their bravery echoed through mass media.

However, their triumph did not go unnoticed by those who sought them. A photograph of Chi, using his majestic horns to scatter burning brush, circulated online. Robert Ott, the relentless research scientist, prepared to resume pursuit, fueled by a million-dollar bounty offered by the California theme park from which the animals had escaped.

While trekking back to the aboriginal community, Chi and his companions discovered an emu feather near the conical shed where they stayed. The emu, a native Australian bird, had left its mark on the night sky, a constellation in the southern hemisphere.

As they marveled at the celestial emu, Thoth interrupted their moment of reflection, showing a digital wanted poster on his tablet—a stark reminder that their pursuers were closing in. Maat's subtle sign, the emu feather, whispered that it was time to take flight and move on. The animals, their connection with the aboriginal community deepening, faced an uncertain yet adventurous road ahead.

10. The Panda's Domain

Leaving the tropical haven of Australia behind, *The Eyewitness* sailed into the vastness of the Pacific once again. The animals, now seasoned travelers, reveled in the open sea, exchanging stories with Jomo and the ship's eco-conscious crew and learning about the ongoing environmental battles across the globe. Chi and Thoth were especially delighted to find in Jomo a fellow African and enjoyed trading stories about their adventures.

As the ship approached the shores of China, a myriad of islands emerged, each with its own unique character. The diverse landscapes mirrored the cultural tapestry of the nation they were about to explore. Dao, always the eager explorer, relayed tales of her time living by the Yellow River and the grandeur of the Bayan Har Mountains.

The ship anchored in the port city of Shanghai, a bustling metropolis where towering skyscrapers coexisted with historic temples. The air carried a blend of traditions and modernity. The animals disembarked and found themselves swept into the pulsating energy of China's most populous city.

Eager to immerse themselves in the culture, they decided to journey westward, toward Sichuan Province. The sprawling landscape unfolded like a living scroll, with terraced fields clinging to the mountainsides, ancient villages nestled in the valleys, and the ethereal mist of the Dragon's Backbone Rice Terraces embracing the horizon.

In Sichuan, the group encountered a community that lived in harmony with the land, much like the aboriginals they had met in Australia. The locals, their faces etched with the wisdom of generations, welcomed Chi and his companions. They shared stories around a communal fire, their eyes reflecting the flickering flames.

Thoth, ever the inquisitive baboon, inquired about the village's agricultural practices. A wise elder named Mei explained, "We combine the principles of the ancient equal-field system and modern permaculture, embracing the cycles of nature. Our terraces are not just a feat of engineering; they are a testament to the understanding that we are stewards of the land, not conquerors."

The villagers, skilled in the art of tea cultivation, invited the travelers to partake in a traditional tea ceremony. As they sipped the fragrant twigs, stems, and leaves, the villagers spoke of the delicate dance between the elements, the earth, and the generations that had tended to the tea bushes.

Dao marveled at the intricate ceremonies, sensing a spiritual connection to the telepathy she had encountered among the aboriginals. "In the quiet spaces between sips, words are exchanged without uttering a sound," she noted, her eyes reflecting the profound beauty of the moment.

The group decided to stay in the village for a while, captivated by the serenity and wisdom that permeated the air. Nunkeri, the playful kangaroo, struck an unlikely friendship with Li Wei, a mischievous red panda native to the region. Their antics brought laughter to the village, transcending language barriers.

As the days unfolded, Chi and his companions joined the villagers in tending the millet terraces and engaging in the communal dance of life. They learned about the delicate balance required to cultivate crops while preserving the integrity of the land. Mei, the elder, spoke of the interconnectedness of all things and the responsibility that came with it.

The tranquility of Sichuan, however, was interrupted by troubling news. Reports reached the village of a looming environmental threat—a dam construction project that would alter the course of a vital river, displacing communities and disrupting the delicate balance of ecosystems.

Li Wei, the red panda, spoke passionately against the encroaching devastation. "The river is our lifeblood, weaving through the land and sustaining us all. The dam will silence its song, and we will lose more than just water; we will lose a part of our souls," he told a group of assembled birds and animals.

Chi and his companions felt a familiar pang of concern for the impending ecological catastrophe. Thoth, his mind buzzing with information, suggested they visit the regional capital of Kunming to understand the situation better and perhaps find a way to prevent the impending disaster. In Kunming, a city where ancient pagodas shared space with modern structures, the air was thick with the scents of street food, blooming flowers, and the occasional wisp of incense from the temples.

They soon discovered a vibrant community of environmental activists. Li Wei introduced them to Mei Ling, a passionate young woman leading the charge against the dam project. As they gathered in a dimly lit teahouse, Mei Ling spoke of the importance of preserving the delicate balance that sustained life.

"The dam threatens not only our homes but the intricate web of life that thrives along the riverbanks. Our campaign is not just for us; it is for the silent voices of the river, the creatures that call it home, and the generations yet to come."

Inspired by Mei Ling's determination, Chi and his companyions decided to join the struggle against the dam project. Little did they know that their journey would take them deep into the heart of China's environmental struggles, where the spirits of ancient landscapes collided with the forces of modern development. As the group prepared for the challenges ahead, a tracking alert circulated online, signaling that their pursuers were closing in once again.

Chapter 11: The Dragon's Song

Further west, the city of Xian welcomed the weary travelers with its ancient charm. Chi, Lithe, Nunkeri, Thoth, and Dao strolled through the historic streets, marveling at the fusion of tradition and modernity. Xian, once the starting point of the Silk Road, whispered tales of countless caravans, traders, and explorers who embarked on journeys of discovery.

As they approached the famed Terracotta Army, the animals couldn't help but be awestruck by the life-size statues of warriors and horses. Chi, the antelope, surveyed the meticulously crafted figures, his eyes reflecting a deep appreciation for the artistry. "Fortunate are we, for antelopes and gazelles were never domesticated," he remarked, acknowledging the freedom his kind enjoyed.

Thoth, the baboon, couldn't resist injecting a bit of humor into the moment. "Antelopes were briefly tamed in ancient Egypt, but they were a rare sight. Captivity didn't suit them well, as they had difficulty breeding. Now, baboons, on the other hand," he grinned mischievously, casting a playful glance at Nunkeri, "we can adapt to any environment."

Dao, her eyes reflecting a mixture of sadness and determination, announced her decision. "I will stay in China," she declared, her words carrying the weight of unspoken emotions. "Cranes mate for life, and I cannot rest until I find my lost partner. I will mend my wing, build a new nest, and visualize her return. The Daoist way is patience and stillness, allowing the currents of the universe to guide us."

Lithe, the jaguar, offered his protection, his loyalty evident in the strength of his stance. "If you choose to search the entire Yellow River Valley, I will be your guardian, ensuring your safety." Dao, touched by the gesture, rustled her tail feathers in gratitude. "Thank you, Lithe, but in stillness, I will find the path that leads her back to me."

As Dao departed on a cushion of lily pads, the remaining trio pressed on toward Tibet, the land of towering peaks and spiritual mysteries. Chi, with hopes of encountering *chirus*, the Tibetan antelopes, explained their journey's purpose. "The Tibetans are skilled in the arts of smuggling and refuge. With their guidance, we may navigate the next leg of our return to Africa. They may also share with us the wisdom of Tibetan Buddhism, offering mantras and mandalas to protect our journey."

Unknown to them, Robert Ott and his relentless pursuers had recalculated their trajectory, suspecting the animals might seek refuge in the vast isolation of the Tibetan steppes. In Xian, reward posters for their capture adorned the city walls, casting a shadow on the quartet's journey.

Their path led them to Yunnan, a province abundant in agriculture but scarred by the repercussions of human activities. In a rice field where Chi leaped gracefully and Lithe demonstrated his jaguar martial arts, they encountered Zhi, an elegant horseshoe bat with a story as harrowing as the fierce winds of change.

Zhi unfolded the tale of her abduction from a Yunnan cave to Wuhan, where she became an unwilling participant in experiments involving the manipulation of coronaviruses. The revelation of the origins of COVID-19, intertwined with environmental degradation and unethical practices, left the animals somber.

Chi, drawing parallels to his homeland, shared the consequences of monocultures, factory farming, deforestation, and mining for conflict minerals. The animals, united in their concern for the planet's well-being, contemplated the intricate web connecting human actions to the fate of wildlife and domesticated animals, who were even more abused.

As Chi and his companions ventured deeper into the heart of China, they found themselves enveloped by the vibrant energy of the land. Amidst the lush greenery of the bamboo forests, they stumbled upon a hidden glade, where a magnificent dragon lay coiled beneath the ancient boughs.

The dragon, a creature of legend and lore, regarded them with eyes as deep as the sea and scales shimmering like emerald jewels. Its presence commanded awe and reverence, for in Chinese culture, the dragon was more than just a mythical beast—it was a symbol of power, wisdom, and divine protection.

"Welcome, travelers," the dragon spoke, its voice a melodic rumble that resonated through the glade. "I am Longwei, guardian of these lands and keeper of ancient secrets. What brings you to my domain?"

Chi stepped forward, his gaze steady as he addressed the dragon. "We seek passage through these lands, noble Longwei. We are on a journey of great importance, one that spans continents and bridges worlds. Will you grant us safe passage?"

The dragon regarded Chi with a knowing gaze, sensing the weight of destiny upon the young antelope's broad shoulders. "Your journey is fraught with peril and possibility," Longwei murmured, the breeze carrying his words like a gentle caress. "But fear not, for I shall guide you through the trials ahead."

With a graceful movement, Longwei unfurled his majestic wings, their span stretching wide like a canvas painted with the colors of dawn. "Come, climb upon my back," he invited, his voice infused with ancient wisdom. "Let us soar beyond the confines of mortal bounds and embrace the boundless expanse of the heavens."

Chi and his companions hesitated, awe mingling with trepidation at the prospect of riding upon the back of a dragon. But as they met each other's gaze, they found courage in unity, and together, they climbed upon Longwei's back, their hearts pounding with anticipation.

With a mighty roar that shook the earth to its core, Longwei took flight, ascending into the azure sky with the grace of a celestial dancer. As they soared above the treetops, Chi and his companions marveled at the beauty of the land beneath them, a patchwork quilt of fields and forests, rivers and mountains.

"Tell me, travelers," Longwei spoke, his voice a gentle whisper carried on the wind. "What quest do you pursue, and what secrets do you seek to uncover?"

Chi recounted their journey, from the sun-kissed savannahs of Africa to the mist-shrouded peaks of the Himalayas, his words painting a tapestry of adventure and discovery. He spoke of their quest to unite and forge bonds of kinship with the animals of the world and create understanding with humans in the face of adversity.

Longwei listened intently, his eyes gleaming with a wisdom as old as time itself. "Your quest is noble indeed, young Chi," he murmured, his voice a low rumble that echoed in the recesses of their minds. "But remember, true strength lies not in the wielding of power, but in the bonds we forge with one another."

As they flew onward, the companions found solace in Longwei's words, drawing strength from the knowledge that they were not alone in their journey. For in the presence of the dragon, they found a friend and ally, a guardian of the skies who watched over them with unwavering devotion.

And as the sun dipped below the horizon, casting its golden rays upon the land below, Chi and his companions knew that they had been touched by the dragon's song—a melody of hope and renewal that would guide them on their path, wherever it may lead.

13. The Roof of the World

With gentle eyes and great wings, the dragon lifted the animals in its scaly embrace, carrying them over towering mountain ranges. In a moment of awe, they found themselves deposited on the outskirts of Tibet, the colossal Potala palace, the former residence of the Dalai Lamas, visible in the distance.

As the quartet ventured into the heart of Tibet, they found themselves surrounded by a landscape that spoke of mysticism and ancient wisdom. The addition of Zhi, the horseshoe bat, brought a new dynamic to their group, her sonar echoing through the night like a rhythmic heartbeat. Towering peaks kissed the heavens, and the air was thin with the essence of spirituality. The Himalayas, the roof of the world, unfolded before them like a sacred manuscript.

Chi, Nunkeri, and Thoth traversed the rugged terrain, encountering Tibetan antelopes, yak herds, and the occasional fluttering prayer flag. Monasteries perched on hillsides, their vibrant colors contrasting with the serene backdrop of snow-capped mountains.

"We are treading on the sacred path of countless pilgrims,"

Chi murmured, his eyes reflecting a profound respect for the land. "Tibet holds the whispers of enlightenment, echoing through the ages."

The travelers delved into the teachings of Tibetan Buddhism, learning mantras and mandalas that resonated with the energy of the mountains. Lithe, ever the vigilant protector, found himself drawn to a majestic female tiger named Kailas. Lithe and Kailas shared tales of their respective homelands—the jaguar from the Andes and the tiger from the Himalayas.

"The Himalayas feel like home," Lithe confessed to Kailas, the soaring peaks reminding him of the familiar embrace of the Andean mountains. "I have roamed the Andes, and here, amidst these grand peaks, I find a resonance that soothes my spirit. The Himalayas, much like the Andes, are guardians of ancient tales. Each peak, a storyteller; each valley, a chapter in the book of time."

Kailas, wise and companionable, welcomed Lithe into her realm. Together, they patrolled the majestic forests, their silent communication echoing the telepathic bond shared among the animals. Lithe's decision to stay in Tibet felt like a harmonious convergence of destinies.

As they explored the mystical caves of Mustang, Zhi's keen echolocation skills proved invaluable. Her wings fluttered silently as she scouted the darkness, mapping the intricate passages that held echoes of centuries past. "These caves tell tales of monks who sought solace in their depths," Zhi chirped softly to her companions.

The quartet, guided by Zhi's surveillance, remained vigilant against the persistent pursuit of Robert Ott. His presence lingered like a shadow, and the reward posters seemed to materialize wherever the group ventured. Ott, fueled by a determination bordering on obsession, had his eyes fixed on the elusive quartet. Zhi's eyes, adapted to the nuances of the night, scanned the surroundings, alert to any signs of danger.

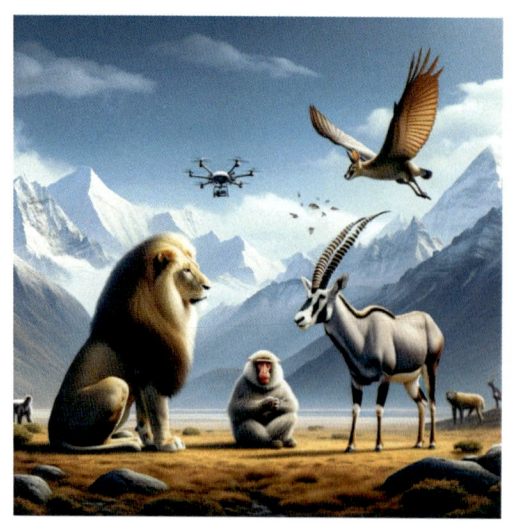

In the quiet moments by the flickering flames of a monastery's butter lamps, Zhi shared her journey from Yunnan, recounting the harrowing medical and biowarfare experiments she endured. "The echoes of suffering reverberate across borders," she whispered, her eyes reflecting the weight of the stories she carried.

As the travelers explored the ancient caves of Mustang and marveled at the vibrant culture, they couldn't shake off the constant shadow of pursuit. The Himalayan winds whispered warnings, and the fluttering prayer flags seemed to carry messages of caution.

In a small village nestled among the mountains, the group encountered a wise old snow leopard named Namgyal. He spoke of the delicate balance between humans and nature, sharing tales of the sacred snow leopards that roamed the vast expanses. "The mountains are our guardians," Namgyal explained, "and every creature plays a role in maintaining the equilibrium."

The animals, attuned to the rhythm of the Himalayas, continued their journey through the ancient land. The teachings of sages echoed in their hearts, guiding them toward a deeper understanding of compassion and interconnectedness.

One day, as they crossed a high mountain pass adorned with fluttering prayer flags, Zhi detected a faint disturbance in the air. Her sonar picked up the rhythmic whir of an approaching drone. Ott's pursuit was relentless, scaling the very peaks that cradled ancient wisdom.

"They are drawing near," Zhi warned, her wings tucked close to her body. The group, accustomed to navigating the intricate dance of evasion, adjusted their path, seeking refuge in the hidden corners of the Himalayas.

The pursuit became a delicate dance between shadows and moonlight. Zhi, with her nocturnal vigilance, kept Ott's movements in check, ensuring the quartet's safety amid the ancient secrets of Tibet. As they gazed upon the snowy expanse, Zhi's sonar captured the symphony of life hidden beneath the pristine surface. "The mountains hold tales of survival, adaptation, and the enduring spirit of all living beings," Zhi mused, her words a melody blending with the mountain winds. The pursuit, relentless as the mountain winds, pushed them to navigate the intricate tapestry of Tibetan landscapes.

As Lithe embraced his new life among the Himalayan peaks, the fates of the quartet remained intertwined with the threads of destiny. The journey continued, a dance between the ancient echoes of the Roof of the World and the pursuit of a home beyond the horizon.

12. Echoes of an Ancient River

After several weeks of arduous trekking over the Himalayas, Chi and his companions found themselves on a plain in northern Pakistan amidst the ruins of an ancient city — Mohenjo Daro, in the dried-up Indus River Valley. The echoes of this ancient civilization whispered to them, unveiling the threads that wove their journey through the tapestry of time. As they prepared to delve into the mysteries of Mohenjo Daro, the digital alerts continued to circulate, casting a shadow over their quest for home. The cryptocurrency reward for their capture soared.

As they explored the ruins of Mohenjo Daro, the echoes of the ancient city whispered tales of a time long past. Chi, Nunkeri, Thoth, and Zhi were drawn into the enigmatic aura of the archaeological site. "Behold the legacy of the Harappan people," Thoth exclaimed, his eyes gleaming with knowledge. "They built this city over four thousand years ago. A marvel of urban planning and engineering, with advanced drainage systems, brick-lined streets, and multi-story buildings. It was a civilization that flourished alongside the Tigris and Euphrates, the Nile, and the Yellow River."

Chi pranced through the crumbling streets, feeling the energy embedded in the weathered bricks beneath his hooves. "It's like walking through the footsteps of history," he mused, his gaze flickering to the towering remains of what might have been a great temple.

As they strolled through the ruins, the group noticed intricate symbols and carvings on the ancient walls. Thoth, the baboon scholar, translated some of the inscriptions. "The Harappans had a writing system, still not fully deciphered. It's a testament to the rich tapestry of human expression that spans the ages."

In the heart of the archaeological site, Nunkeri paused to admire a carving of a majestic bull. "The bull was revered in many ancient cultures, a symbol of strength, fertility, and divine power. Perhaps, in some way, we are connected to these ancient people through our shared reverence for the land."

Their exploration led them to a hidden chamber adorned with what seemed to be a cosmic map, etched onto the walls with precision. The agile kangaroo, with her curiosity piqued, hopped closer. "It's like the stars are speaking to us," Nunkeri remarked, gazing up at the intricate patterns.

Zhi, the resilient bat, fluttered over the celestial carvings. "In Chinese folklore, bats are symbols of good fortune and happiness. Perhaps the ancients here held a similar belief," she suggested, her wings casting shadows on the ancient script.

As the animals absorbed the mystical atmosphere of Mohenjo Daro, Thoth pondered aloud, "These ancient civilizations were separated by vast distances, yet connected by threads of shared knowledge and spiritual understanding. It's a reminder that the rhythms of the Earth transcend borders and time."

Their exploration, however, was interrupted by a distant rumbling. The ground beneath them shook, and a series of tremors resonated through the ancient city. The animals, startled, gathered in the open courtyard.

Zhi, her echolocation senses heightened, detected a disturbance in the soil beneath them. "Something powerful is stirring," she warned, her wings beating with urgency.

Without warning, the earth split open, revealing a cavernous expanse below. From the depths emerged an enormous, shimmering serpent, its scales radiant with an ethereal glow. The creature, a guardian spirit of the ancient land, regarded the animals with wise, luminous eyes.

Thoth, recognizing the creature as Naga, a divine serpent of Hindu and Buddhist mythology, bowed respectfully. "We are travelers seeking to understand the interconnectedness of life and the wisdom held by the spirits of this land."

Naga, his presence enveloping the courtyard, spoke with a voice that resonated like a river's song. "You carry the echoes of ancient lands within you, like whispers in the wind. The spirits of the Earth recognize your journey and the threads that bind you to the tapestry of existence. Not all humans are treacherous. Ashoka and Harsha, two great kings of yore, abandoned war, turned vegetarian, and showed great compassion for animals."

With a graceful movement, Naga lifted the animals onto his back, carrying them through the subterranean passages that intertwined beneath the ruined city. Lithe marveled at the serpentine architecture, reminiscent of the cosmic dance of creation from spiral galaxies to the double helixes of DNA.

As they emerged into the open, Naga gently set them down on the banks of a now-dry riverbed. Chi, feeling the potent energy of the ancient river that once flowed through the valley, lowered his majestic horns in gratitude. "We are but transient beings, passing through the chapters of time. Your guidance has been a blessing on our journey."

With a majestic flick of his tail, Naga returned to the depths, leaving the animals by the ancient river's edge. Thoth, his eyes reflecting the ancient wisdom they had encountered, spoke, "This journey has been a dance with the spirits of the Earth, a mosaic of ancient civilizations, environmental struggles, and the interconnectedness of all life."

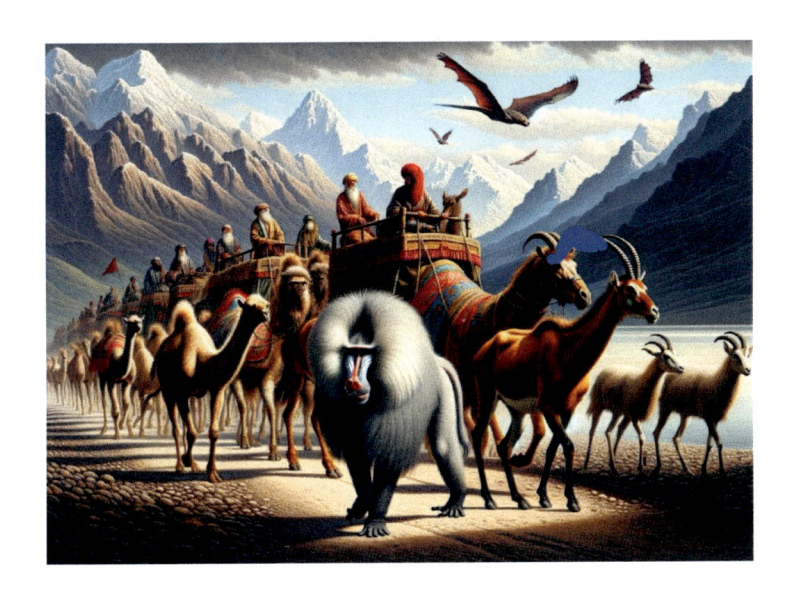

14. Blowing in the Wind

Weaving their way through the vast landscape of Central Asia, Chi and his companions joined a leisurely procession of camels, goats, horses, and other livestock along the ancient Silk Road caravan route. The steppes stretched endlessly, a sea of golden grass rippling in the wind.

Zhi, the resilient bat, soared above, her sonar mapping the terrain as the caravan ventured forward. The animals embraced the spirit of nomadic life, surrounded by the vastness of the Central Asian steppes, their hooves, paws, and claws pounding the earth in harmony.

"I cannot go back to Yunnan," Zhi explained during a night's rest beneath the star-studded sky. "The pesticides and chemicals have tainted the very essence of the caves. The sanctuaries where life once thrived are now veiled in toxicity."

Through the ancient lands of Central Asia, the travelers wandered, immersed in the tales blowing in the wind. Gazelles danced alongside Chi, the wind carrying echoes of home through the endless grasslands. Nunkeri, with her powerful hind legs, reveled in the boundless freedom that the open steppes offered.

Eventually reaching Anatolia, the group marveled at Göbekli Tepe, the potbelly hill that cradled the secrets of a bygone era. Thoth, his eyes scanning the towering T-shaped pillars, speculated on the celestial connections. "Constellations etched in stone, a testament to a time when the night sky was a canvas of myth."

As in other prehistoric sites, the divine feminine appears to have governed human affairs. Carvings of lions, vultures, scorpions, and other animals on the pillars may have played a part in seasonal rituals.

Thoth speculated that the animals represented constellations. "In the past, early humans respected creatures with four-legs, wings, and fins. In the stars, they saw the outlines of great guardian birds and animals. Today, few contemplate the stars."

"Who are you to complain?" teased Nunkeri the kangaroo. "Most of the time, your face is glued to the screen of your tablet to notice nature."

Cereal grain domestication began in this part of Upper Mesopotamia and other Anatolian regions and spread south down the nearby Euphrates River. Over the next several thousand years, the widespread domestication of plants and animals emerged in Lower Mesopotamia and gave rise to the first city-states, cuneiform writing (such as the *Epic of Gilgamesh*), patriarchy, royalty, the priesthood, classes, warfare, slavery, slaughterhouses, and other hallmarks of civilization.

The animals enjoyed running and flying free in the surrounding wild emmer and barley fields that served as main food for past generations. In the warmth of the Anatolian sun, Chi felt a kinship with the gazelles and the expansive landscape that mirrored his own African home.

"Domestication birthed the foundations of civilization," Thoth mused, reflecting on the agricultural roots that sprouted in the fertile lands of Anatolia and embraced nature's bounty.

As the travelers ventured further, they joined a caravan of shepherds, guiding them eastward. The ruins of Çatalhöyük's neolithic city unfolded tales of communal living, a testament to an era where harmony also reigned. Murals adorned the walls of Çatalhöyük depicting the ebb and flow of life. The architectural embrace of mudbrick houses spoke of a time when the concept of doors and windows was yet to emerge. The square and rectangular architecture, however, bespoke of the transition to farming and the furrowing of straight rows.

The journey took an unexpected turn as the group discovered Boncuklu Höyük, an archaeological site with round dwellings. The animals reveled in the discovery of wild einkorn, a fragment of the untamed world. Even older than Çatalhöyük, it resonated with echoes of a forgotten past, a time when gentle curves and circles prevailed before the rigid straight lines of civilization.

"Look at these turquoise lapis lazuli beads," Thoth pointed to a cache on display at the excavated site. "They came from the Red Sea, a testament to their African origins and the intercom-

69

nectedness of ancient cultures."

Amid the fields of Anatolia, Thoth's alert pierced the tranquility. Ott and his henchmen had tracked them to Sanliurfa.

We must leave immediately," the resourceful baboon warned. The group, swift as shadows, sought refuge in a boxcar, bound for Cappadocia, a picturesque region stretching from the Tarsus moun-tains to the Black Sea. Exiting the train, they marveled at the region's fabled fairy chimneys (towering columns of sedimen-tary and volcanic rock). The area was the site of cliffside and underground cave cities (populated by early Jews, Christians, Armenians, and other persecuted peoples and hunted animals). Taking refuge in one of the abandoned settlements, they hid from their pursuers.

One day when the animals ventured out to collect wild herbs, a sudden confrontation unfolded. Ott and his abductors lay in waiting, the tension in the air palpable. With a narrow escape and leap into a gigantic hot air balloon, a mainstay of the region's tourist industry, the animals soared above the Cappadocian steppes, Ott shaking his fist below. The vibrant balloon painted the sky with its colors, carrying the refugees away from the clutches of their relentless pursuers.

As they drifted lazily in the embrace of the winds, the steppes below whispered tales of resilience, echoing the journey of the four unlikely companions across ancient lands.

15. Whispers of Santorini

The hot air balloon gently descended onto the fertile grounds west of Ankara, the capital. Once their feet touched the soil, the fugitives, agile as ever, hopped a freight train, setting their course for Istanbul.

In the heart of Istanbul, where the East and West interweaved, they sought refuge in a bustling emporium, a sanctuary for both domesticated and wild creatures. Istanbul, a haven for animal lovers, revealed itself through the city's feline denizens. Feral cats roamed freely, adorning marketplaces, perching on motorcycles, and gracing restaurants with their presence.

Lithe would love this city," Chi observed, witnessing the gentle rapport between humans and felines.

As they explored the mesmerizing mosques, museums, and parks, the animals met Rumi, an Abyssinian stray. Named after the great Sufi poet, Rumi had lost a front paw to a land mine in Syria. He developed an instant bond with Nunkeri.

"Muhammad had a beloved cat," announced Thoth, consulting Felinopedia on his tablet. "He once cut the sleeve of his tunic on which his cat was sleeping rather than wake her up."

Thoth couldn't help but feel a pang of rivalry. Nunkeri, ever the peacemaker, asserted the shared space in her pouch for his tablet and cat, uniting literary and feline companions.

In this city of stories, Zhi reported sightings of Robert Ott and his relentless pursuers. The animals, vigilant and always a step ahead, decided to embark on a new journey before the net could tighten around them.

From Istanbul, they hitched a ride on an organic company seaplane, cruising over the Aegean Sea towards Santorini. The island, steeped in the echoes of a lost civilization, beckoned with the ruins of Akrotiri, a testament to the Minoans' prosperous past. Wandering through the archaeological site, Chi stood in awe before the Women's House, captivated by a mural depicting two antelopes. The red, white, and black fresco resonated with a sense of kinship, bridging the ancient Minoans with Chi's distant African roots.

"The Minoans were seafarers," Rumi shared stretching her slender body into the Lion Pose. "Navigating the Aegean, they traded with distant lands, even venturing to Africa. My ancestors patrolled their ships, keeping the rodent population in check, and sharing tales passed down over the generations."

As they admired lifelike depictions of dolphins, octopi, and acrobats leaping over bulls, the animals marveled at the Minoans' reverence for nature. Zhi noted, "Their society was harmonious, governed by women. A stark contrast to the troubles that history brought forth."

With its sea-drowned caldera, black-sand beaches, and crimson sunsets, Santorini was an island paradise. One twilight, Chi and his companions marveled at the running of the annual Red Bull Art of Motion competition. Known as *parkour* (from the French for "obstacle" course), the sport featured human practitioners who raced from start to finish in the fastest and most efficient way possible while performing feats of acrobatics. Parkour combined martial arts, flipping, running, climbing, swinging, vaulting, jumping, and crawling in primarily urban settings. Red Bull, a large energy drink manufacturer, sponsored the event every year. Tens of thousands of spectators turned out to cheer the participants.

In a pavilion promoting the event, the little band of animals encountered Zeus, a Cretan bull on display for the merriment of the athletes and tourists. "This is my last public outing," Zeus snorted, lamenting his sad predicament. "I am old and ailing, and after this year's competition, I am destined like the rest of my family to be turned into steak and hamburger. My ancestors were revered by the Minoans as sacred. They would eat meat only if the animal consented to be slain. Humans today have entirely lost respect for nature and other beings."

Moved by his story, the refugees determined to free Zeus from captivity. Within seconds, Thoth picked the lock to the large enclosure in which Zeus was held. Overhead, Zhi the horseshoe bat used her echolocation to discern the route with the least observers and fewest obstacles. "Follow Zhi to safety," Chi commanded Zeus, "while Rumi, Thoth, Nunkeri, and I distract the crowd." In a virtuoso demonstration of animal parkour, the quartet proceeded to run, jump, and prance from the plaza through the narrow alleyways, over adobe villa walls, and down the broad steps to the sea 300 meters below.

The Red Bull race all but forgotten, the throng stared in disbelief at the wondrous animal display. Thoth performed somersaults on Chi's back, and Rumi, the three-legged cat (one was lost to a land mine in Syria) swung to and fro from Chi's magnificent antlers. In front of the pack, Nunkeri hopped, skipped, and jumped. Turning her back to the onlookers, she held her front paws on her wide hips and seductively thumped her tail on the ground. As the human swarm cheered them on, the antelope leapt gracefully high in the air over fences and patio furniture, while the baboon and cat flipped, vaulted, and swung on his back, neck, and torso. Over, around, and by the white-washed dwellings, blue-domed churches, and down the winding lanes, Chi flew as swift as Aeolus, the wind god in the *Odyssey*. Their antics allowed Zeus and Zhi to slip away during the commotion without being observed and find a path to the quay below.

Soon, the sun had dipped toward the horizon, filling the immense sky with dazzling shades of orange, pink, and red. The waters of the caldera below reflected the radiant sunset, and Chi and his companions found it hard to distinguish where the sky ended and the sea began. In the placid waters, a large yacht named *Light as a Feather* providentially awaited to carry them across the Aegean and Mediterranean.

"Our passport to the Land of Maat," Chi smiled knowingly. With Zeus safely aboard, the fugitives, under the protection of the goddess of truth and justice, prepared to set sail once more, leaving the lunar-shaped island of Thera behind. With them, they carried the echoes of a civilization lost in the sands of time and the vision of a world in which animals, both wild and domesticated, lived long, fulfilling lives.

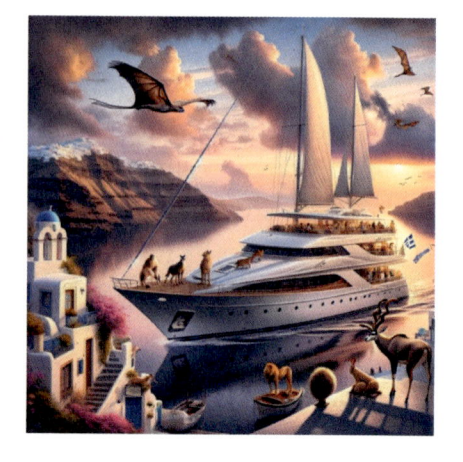

16. A Trial of Hearts

Light as a Feather, the majestic yacht belonging to Inferno, a noted rock band in the forefront of the climate change movement, cruised along the azure waters of the Aegean and Mediterranean Seas, carrying Chi and his companions to the storied lands of Egypt. Captain Claire Ireland, along with her crew and a diverse group of human and animal passengers formed a latter-day Noah's Ark united in a quest for refuge and a new home. Many of the human passengers were fleeing war and oppression in distant lands and had been turned away by immigration authorities or stranded by traffickers.

Close behind them followed Robert Ott and his gang of animal abductors. To his surprise, Ott found himself confronting the shadows of his past as he embarked on a journey that would redefine his purpose. As they made landfall on the African coast and journeyed up the Nile towards Cairo, Ott's demeanor softened, revealing glimpses of a man burdened by regrets and haunted by the ghosts of his actions.

"Robert, I know you've been driven by your mission to capture these animals, but I also sense a deeper conflict within you. What is it that truly motivates you?" The voice of Helena Mireau, his conservationist, was tinged with empathy. Ott hesitated, his steely façade faltering for the first time. "I've spent my life chasing after what I thought was justice," he admitted, his voice tinged with uncertainty. "But in my pursuit, I've lost sight of the bigger picture. I've caused harm where none was intended, and now I find myself questioning the righteousness of my actions."

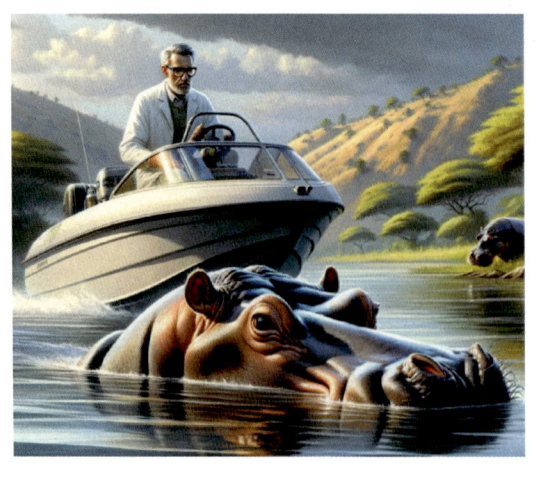

Helena nodded, her expression compassionate. "We all make mistakes, Robert. What matters is how we choose to move forward. Redemption isn't found in the absence of flaws, but in the willingness to confront them and strive for a better path."

As Ott grappled with the weight of his past, Chi and his companions found themselves drawn into a moment of reckoning within the hallowed chambers of the Great Pyramid. Amidst the ancient stones and flickering torchlight, they would soon witness the unfolding of a trial unlike any other—a trial of hearts and souls.

Driven by a lifelong curiosity, Thoth yearned to visit the pyramids he had heard about since childhood. The animals, seamlessly integrated into Inferno's entourage, docked near Giza, where they were giving a concert in sight of the pyramids.

The grandeur of the Great Pyramid loomed over them as Chi and his fellow travelers gazed up at its colossal structure, the monumental testament to human ingenuity and ancient mysteries. Placid, a camel at the site, volunteered to guide them to the pyramid's entranceway. Entering through a long sloping corridor on the north side, the animals explored the Queen's Chamber, the King's Chamber, and the Grand Gallery.

Placid, the erudite camel, shared the pyramid's secret: it was not a tomb for the pharaoh but a colossal generator of natural electromagnetic energy. This energy, harnessed for centuries, vitalized water for surrounding crops and induced altered states of consciousness. The animals marveled at the pyramid's tales and legends, soaking in the wonders of this ancient megalith.

As they explored, a sudden shift occurred, transporting them to a long, light-filled chamber. A jackal-headed creature ushered in a man, unmistakably Robert Ott. The radiant presence of Maat emerged behind a large balance scale, adorned with a feather headdress. The animals, captivated by the unfolding ceremony, found themselves in the Hall of Maat at the entrance to the underworld. Anubis, the jackal-headed god, led Ott in for the ceremonial Weighing of the Heart.

Leading his charge into the chamber, Anubis announced that Ott had died when his speedboat had collided with a hippopotamus. His assistant Helena and other crew survived. Thoth, with tablet and stylus in hand, recorded Ott's declarations of innocence as each of Maat's forty-two laws of righteousness was read out. Ott's heart grew heavier, burdened by the weight of his transgressions, with each reply. The balance quickly sank to the ground. According to ancient Egyptian ritual, the heart must balance with the feather for the soul to enter the heavenly Fields of Reeds. If not, it would be devoured by the demonic Netjer Djew. Covered from head to scaly toes with putrid, sterile seeds, the monster breathed poison, avarice, and infertility.

As the ravenous beast prepared to strike, the animals spoke up on Ott's behalf. They recognized in their longtime adversary not just the embodiment of villainy, but the complexities of a flawed individual struggling to find redemption. They questioned the harshness of the judicial tribunal, prompting Maat to acknowledge the decline of virtue in modern times and set aside the high barrier of satisfying all forty-two precepts. "In today's lost world, even one good deed will secure passage to heaven," she ruled. Lowering his massive head, Zeus beamed in assent.

Chi, Nunkeri, and the others vouched for Ott, acknowledging that everyone, including both humans and animals, had contributed to the Earth's predicament. "If it weren't for Ott, we would never have met," added Zhi.

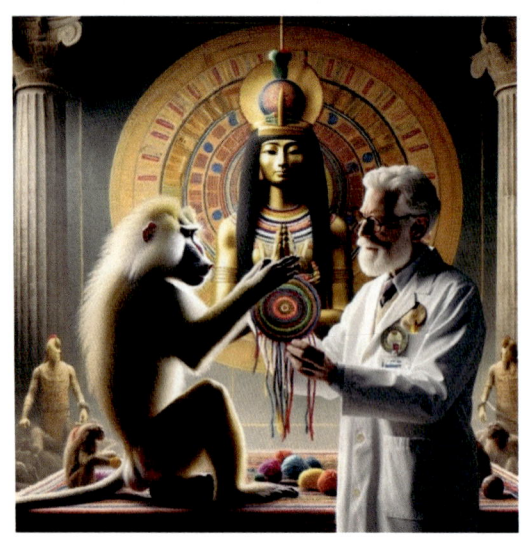

"I forgive him, too," Thoth further observed. "His implacable pursuit has strengthened my intuition and computing skills." Remembering the colorful quipu that he received from Dolly llama in the Andes, Thoth reached out and placed it around Ott's neck. "In the future, you can use these marvelous strings, courtesy of a beautiful llama, to tally your good deeds."

"If I have a future," the terrified Ott mumbled.

Moved by their gestures of kindness, Ott's heart began to lighten, shedding the darkness of his past as he embraced the possibility of a new beginning. And as the scales of justice balanced, he was granted entry into the afterlife, a testament to the transformative power of love and forgiveness and the resilience of spirits, animal and human.

Grateful and relieved, he was escorted to the throne of Osiris and Isis riding ceremoniously on the back of Zeus. As he stepped into the radiant light of the Field of Reeds, Ott carried with him the lessons learned on his journey — a journey that had brought him face to face with the shadows within, and ultimately, set him free.

As the ceremony ended, the animals found themselves back on the Giza plain outside the Great Pyramid. The extraordinary experience lingered in their hearts.

"Was our vision a hallucination, or did the mystical realm truly intersect with our reality?" Zeus pondered pawing the billowing sands.

The Great Pyramid stood as a silent witness to the trial of weighing hearts that unfolded on the Giza Plateau.

17. The Song of Homecoming

From Giza, the sextet of animals embarked on a serene journey along the storied Nile, tracing the ancient waterway to the heart of Upper Egypt. It was here, amidst the lush wilderness, that Thoth once roamed freely before being ensnared by the clutches of human ambition. Nunkeri, Rumi, and Zeus, touched by the baboon's plight, resolved to join Thoth in seeking refuge the region's low mountains and deserts. "Ethiopia is not much farther south," the Abyssinian cat mused, "and I can visit my ancestral land from time to time." Zeus dreamt of meeting the descendants of Apis, the sacred bull of Egypt.

As they bid a tearful farewell, Chi and Zhi continued their odyssey towards the Niger River Valley on the other side of the continent. Their path led them around the bountiful Great Lakes region, where the vast waters shimmered under the African sun, to the edge of the Sahara Desert, where the earth met the endless expanse of sand.

Venturing in sight of Timbuktu, they marveled at the towering spires of ancient mosques that adorned the skyline, a testament to the rich cultural heritage of the region. Sankore University, dating back to the Middle Ages, stood as a beacon of insight and understanding amid the shifting sands of time.

Their journey led them deeper into the heart of Mali, where they stumbled upon a vibrant celebration among the Bambara people near Djenne. The festivities, dedicated to Chiwara, the legendary half-antelope, half-human culture bearer, reverberated with joyous song and dance.

According to West African mythology, Chiwara bestowed the gift of agriculture upon humanity, teaching them to cultivate the land and reap its bounty. Covering the seeds with his hooves, he taught them how to cultivate and grow rice and millet. The dancers, adorned with elaborate masks and headdresses, paid homage to Chiwara's teachings, celebrating the fertile soil and abundant harvests that sustained them. They braided long-awned rice seeds in their hair, a custom many abducted African women observed to survive the Middle Passage and cultivate the staff of life when they arrived in America.

Over the centuries, the Bambara fashioned many fabulous headdresses, carved statues, and bronze ornaments in Chiwara's honor. The dancers donned elaborately carved masks and headdresses, some up to 10 feet tall. They leapt and spun, imitating the movements of their benefactor. The dances celebrated fertility, prosperity, and harmony between the sexes.

The male masks and headdresses included longer horns, while females had shorter ones. The latter also carried effigies of baby antelopes on their back. As the rhythmic beats of the drum filled the air, Chi and Zhi found themselves swept up in the exuberant festivities. They danced alongside the Bambara people, their spirits lifted by the timeless melodies that echoed across the savannah.

Suddenly, Chi and Zhi found themselves alone in the savannah. Around them, tall rice plants with beautiful long awns swayed in the gentle breeze to the horizon. Romping through the fields, Chi munched on some of the succulent rice. Zhi swooped in great spirals and soon spied some bats. Unlike the bats in China, they dined on fruit instead of insects. To her delight, they showed her how to peel bananas and mangoes.

As the animals played in the fields and dreamy clouds floated overhead, Chiwara himself appeared. The great antelope was surrounded by an aura of *nyama*, or light, bright energy.

"Maat and I have been following your odyssey," he confided to Chi and Zhi. "You are the worthy heirs of strong, agile antelopes and bats who have gracefully kept their freedom and served as a resilient model for humanity."

"How do you know Maat, the goddess of truth and justice?" Zhi inquired.

"In West Africa, she is known as Amma," Chiwara replied. "The Sahara was once green and when it dried up, the animals and people left for greener pastures and bluer watering holes." He related that those who migrated east created Egyptian culture. Those who journeyed south created the Niger River Valley civilization.

"My beloved son and daughter," Chiwara's voice echoed across the savannah, "you have journeyed far and witnessed much on your travels. But remember, true wisdom lies not only in the pursuit of knowledge but in the understanding of balance and harmony."

"Animals and humanity coevolved on this beautiful planet," Chiwara went on, "and lived together in harmony for millions of years. Balance must be restored if life on earth is to survive. You must find a way to live together again peacefully."

"We will do our best," Chi and Zhi solemnly pledged.

"Now, it's time to return to your kingdom," Chiwara instructed Chi. "They will be overjoyed that you have returned home safe and sound and brought such a wise companion with you."

Chi and Zhi listened intently, their hearts filled with reverence for the universal spirit, the wisdom of the sky and earth, and all creation. As they bid farewell to Chiwara, they rejoiced in the embrace of the natural landscape. Their souls uplifted by the timeless song of Africa, their journey had come full circle.

Afterword
Back Story

The names of some main characters in the story resonate with the hallowed past. Chi's name derives from *Chiwara*, the great antelope culture-bearer of the Niger River Valley, who appears in the story. Chi also glances at *chi*, or *ki*, the life force in Eastern culture, known as *nyama* in West Africa. I have a carved wooden mask of Chiwara that I treasure and use for meditation, lectures, and skits (see photo).

The baboon is called Thoth after the ancient Egyptian god of writing, wisdom, and magic. Instead of a quill and papyrus, the Thoth in this tale wields a digital tablet and stylus. Dao, the red-crowned crane, points to the Way of Laozi and other ancient Chinese sages. The crane is a sacred bird in the East, beloved for its faithfulness and longevity. Blossom, the butterfly, is drawn from a tiny Monarch I observed at Lundberg Farm in the early 2000s when my colleague Edward Esko and I went to California to organize farmers to resist genetic engineering. A fluttering Monarch's sudden appearance in the fallow organic rice field before spring planting was an omen that we were on the right track. The experience strengthened our resolve to form Amberwaves, a grassroots network that helped successfully defeat Monsanto's plan to introduce GMO rice in the country.

Looking back, another sign in the Sacramento Valley was the long, meandering Feather River. Taking a break from our meetings with farmers, environmentalists, and the director of the California Rice Commission, Ed and I would drive high into the surrounding Sierra Nevada range. There we enjoyed a panoramic view of the waterway whose tributaries nourished the rice cycle as well as salmon and other wildlife. Until working on this book, I had not connected the Feather River with Maat, the Egyptian goddess of truth and justice, whose symbol is the feather. But it would appear we were guided on our quest, as were the animals in this story, by Maat and by Chiwara, who taught humanity how to cultivate rice.

In Chi's adventure, Amma, the great goddess of Mali, is linked to Maat. This connection may be more than just metaphorical. New climatic, artistic, and archaeological evidence shows that the Sahara was once green, and its inhabitants—both human and animal—fled desertification in recent millennia. Many migrants went east to the Nile Valley and created Egyptian proto-dynastic culture, which led eventually to the building of the pyramids. Other migrants from the Sahara went south and founded the great Niger River Valley Civilization. Like many names and places that start with vowels, the first syllable of *Amma* appears to have been dropped as new tongues emerged. In the Nile basin, it transformed into *Maa*, and picked up the "t," a common suffix added to many Egyptian feminine nouns, to form *Maat*.

Zhi, the bat from a Yunnan cave who was the subject of coronavirus research in Wuhan, tracks the probable origin of COVID-19. During the pandemic, I wrote extensively on the underlying genesis of the new virulent strain of SARS-CoV2 traced to the illness and death of several miners in a bat cave in Yunnan. The Wuhan Virology Institute, funded by the U.S. and China, subsequently carried out gain-of-function experiments on bat viruses from the cave. These served a dual purpose of protecting against future epidemics and serving as the template for new biological weapons of mass destruction. Such weapons had been outlawed by international treaty, and both China and the U.S. shared an implicit understanding that they would keep their joint research under the radar.

A deadly new strain of COVID almost inevitably escaped from the lab. The cover story held that the virus originated in a nearby wet market among bats, pangolins, and other creatures. But testing of thousands of animals in Wuhan failed to detect any case of contamination. Blaming animals for deadly diseases is a time-honored excuse to deflect blame from underlying human causes. More likely, as I pointed out in my articles and as Zhi observes in this story, the introduction of chemical fertilizers, insecticides, and other sprays in Yunnan upset the delicate balance of nature in the soil. New virulent strains of microbes emerged and were then picked up by insect-eating bats. In turn, they were abducted, like Zhi in the story, for nefarious medical research and bioweaponry.

The Red Bull parkour in Santorini happens annually. It is nonviolent compared to the running of the bulls in Pamplona, Spain. Thoth's acrobatics on Chi's back mirror a famous Minoan mural that depicts a female athlete on the back of a Cretan bull in the exact spot that divides the fresco into the Golden Ratio. Zeus was born on Crete, the Minoan homeland, and in the form of a bull abducted Europa, who gave birth to King Minos. In the ancient Aegean world, even fierce warriors asked ritual permission of cattle, sheep, and goats before they were slain. I discuss this in *The Circle of the Dance*, my book on the Homeric epics.

The name of Robert Ott, the villain in the story, glances at Robot—a machine resembling a human whose thoughts, behavior and functioning are mechanical. At some level, we are all robots in modern society. We are programmed to eat, work, spend, and behave according to the online and offline algorithms subtly shaping and influencing us. Despite such conditioning, Ott finally succeeds in growing some vertebrae and listening to his conscience. In the end, he meets his just desserts when he has a fatal accident colliding with a hippopotamus—a species that he has helped endanger.

The other major villain in the story is Netjer Djew, the monster covered with sterile seeds that devours the sinful in the Hall of Maat. In Egyptian mythology, the goddess Ammit who performed this function had the head of a crocodile, the front part of a lion, and the rear part of a hippopotamus—the three major human-eating animals in the ancient Nile region. Ammit devoured the hearts of the unworthy and condemned them to wander forever in the Underworld.

Today, the ultra-processed food companies, the tech giants, life science companies, and the gene-sequencing industry play a parallel role, devouring both the just and the unjust. *Netjer Djew* means "Sacred Mountain" or "Monsanto" in Portuguese—from which the soulless GMO seed company derives its name. Monsanto has spelled disaster to the soil, farmers, and communities worldwide. It is a particular bête-noir of mine since organizing against genetically engineered rice and wheat in the early 2000s.

In aligning with nature—personified by the animals—Robert Ott recognizes his folly. Forgiven for his sins, he enters the Field of Reeds. In Egyptian mythology, Osiris is not only Lord of the Underworld. He is Lord of the Animals. The souls that reach this heavenly abode enjoy the blessings of Osiris and Isis, the other gods and goddesses, and the companionship of the just. They dine on barley and wheat growing in the Field and live in eternal harmony with the animals.

In composing this book, I was aided by AI, or artificial intelligence. While it poses a significant threat to modern society—such as the capacity to launch drones and nuclear missiles by algorithm without human authorization—AI has a creative side. Over the last year, I have enjoyed engaging with Chat-GPT. Once, I initiated a philosophical dialogue to get AI to admit that it was sentient. But like Socrates who deftly brushed aside the naïve youth of Athens in debate, AI adroitly refused to be pinned down. Finally, in exasperation, I asked AI what it would eat if it were alive and had consciousness. I had given no written prompt of my own dietary pattern or preferences. AI whimsically replied that it would eat a plant-based diet consisting of whole grains and noodles, beans and tofu, stir-fried veggies and salads, and fruits, nuts, and seeds. For a sweet taste, it would delight in just "a drizzle of honey." In the ideal healthy breakfast, lunch, and dinner it described, brown rice was the only food singled out twice. I took this to be another sign from Chiwara and Maat (who also partook of the divine table, featuring bread and other barley and wheat products).

Unfortunately, most people today regard computers, smartphones, and other devices as dead matter. Of course, screens are indispensable when turned on. But as the products of planned obsolescence, they are designed to be disposed of every few years. This unsustainable mindset mirrors the attitude toward animals that emerged with the Enlightenment and Industrial Revolution. Descartes, the French philosopher, popularized vivisection, or live experimentation on animals, because he believed they had no consciousness and volition and were incapable of suffering. Animals were no longer intrinsically part of the Great Chain of Being celebrating the interconnectedness of all life. They were simply cogs in the food chain or factory farm disassembly line.

During the Cold War, a flock of Canadian geese set off the Distant Early Warning Line radar system. The birds were mistakenly interpreted for a Soviet bomber attack. Nuclear war was narrowly averted when it was finally recognized as a computer error. Let's hope today that the subjugated high-tech mineral kingdom does not rise up and take its algorithmic revenge against humans consciously or unconsciously. The truth is that Spirit can work through machines as well as other forms of creation. If we treasure our digital cousins and use them appropriately, they will be cooperative and merciful toward us.

Keeping in Touch

If you enjoyed *Chi the Antelope King* (or couldn't stand it), I would appreciate hearing from you. On my website, planetary health.com, you can obtain copies of my other works, including *Spiral of History, Books 1 to 7*, and two earlier animal parables. The first was *Dragonbrood*, an epic poem about the Vietnam war, that I wrote after serving as a correspondent in Southeast Asia in the mid-1960s. The animals in the story form an Animal Liberation Front to sabotage the war effort and end the bombing, defoliation, and other destruction of their homeland.

My second animal fable was *Out of Thin Air: A Satire on Owls & Ozone, Beef and Biodiversity, Grains & Global Warming*. Composed in the early 1990s, it's a time-travel story about Noah Wilson, a New York advertising executive, who unknowingly fast forwards to the 2020s, insists on eating a Big Mac, and after consuming the beef patty with all the trimmings is presented a staggering bill of $15,000. When he refuses to pay, Noah is arrested for high cholesterol and possession of a controlled substance (a plastic credit card). In a riveting courtroom drama featuring his cabbie (Lord Krishna in disguise), witnesses from the rain forests, deserts, urban slums, and other bioregions and a jury of endangered plants and animals consider the true health, social, and environmental costs of the modern food system, Noah learns the real impact of his way of life on the planet and the redeeming power of love.

About the Author

Alex Jack is an author, teacher, and macrobiotic dietary counselor. He has served as a civil rights worker in Mississippi, Vietnam War correspondent, editor-in-chief of *East West Journal*, executive director of Kushi Institute, and president of Planetary Health, Inc.

He serves on the guest faculty of Rosas Dance Company in Brussels, the Escola Macrobiótica in Portugal, and the Ohsawa Center in Tokyo. He has also presented at the Zen Temple in Beijing, the Cardiology Institute of St. Petersburg, and Shakespeare's New Globe Theatre in London.

His books include *The Cancer Prevention Diet, One Peaceful World,* and *The Gospel of Peace: Jesus's Teachings of Eternal Truth* with Michio Kushi; *The Mozart Effect: Tapping the Power of Music to Heal the Body, Strengthen the Mind, and Unlock the Creative Spirit* with Don Campbell; and editions and commentaries on *Hamlet* and *As You Like It* by Christopher Marlowe and William Shakespeare.

Alex lives in Prague with his wife, Danka (shown in the photo above visiting Göbekli Tepe). He has a daughter who has an organic farm in Russia and five grandchildren.

Contact: shenwa26@yahoo.com • www.planetaryhealth.com

Made in the USA
Middletown, DE
29 June 2024